"My name is Stratemeier."

The horseman glanced from the dark-skinned Naco to the fat white man. "I'm looking for Boone Shields."

"You've found him," the white man thundered. He turned to the saloon doors. "Come on in."

The Indian remained on the porch, hesitant. Stratemeier said, "Go ahead, Naco."

Inside, Stratemeier settled his tall frame in a battered chair. Shields filled a fresh glass and slid it across the table to the newcomer.

"You're the one just bought up most of the Antelope range," Shields said.

"If Hatchet's most of it."

The fat man said: "You're smart, coming to me first."

"I like to know who I'm going to have to fight," Stratemeier said.

THE ARIZONANS

.

Brian Garfield

BANTAM BOOKS

TORONTO · NEW YORK · LONDON · SYDNEY · AUCKLAND

THE ARIZONANS

*A Bantam Book / published by arrangement with
the author*

PRINTING HISTORY
First published in December 1961
Bantam edition / March 1987

ISBN 0-553-26286-6

Published simultaneously in the United States and Canada

*Bantam Books are published by Bantam Books, Inc. Its trademark,
consisting of the words "Bantam Books" and the portrayal of a
rooster, is Registered in U.S. Patent and Trademark Office and in
other countries. Marca Registrada. Bantam Books, Inc., 666 Fifth
Avenue, New York, New York 10103.*

PRINTED IN THE UNITED STATES OF AMERICA

O   0 9 8 7 6 5 4 3 2 1

AUTHOR'S NOTE

The long history of Arizona is penned in considerable blood, beginning in water wars between Indian villages of a thousand years ago and flowing on past the abortive invasions of armored *conquistadores*. While the Union fought the Confederacy, Arizona was fighting Indians; while the Secret Order of the Knights of Labor fought Eastern railroads, in Arizona the Earps fought the Clantons and John Slaughter shotgunned a finish to the job of cleaning up Tombstone. The Hashknife outfit fought off the sheepmen and rustlers (almost synonymously evil in the terms of the times), and peace officers from Fred White to Ben McKinney chased villains from the Apache Kid to John Dillinger and beyond.

Pearl Hart and Big Nose Kate Fisher (or Elder—take your pick); Doc Holliday and Buckskin Frank Leslie; Curly Bill Graham (or Brocious) and the McLowery brothers, Frank and Tom; Burt Alvord and silk-tongued John Ringo; the train-robbing Smith brothers (who rustled Hashknife cattle for a pastime between train jobs) and murdering Augustin Chacon; bandit Billy Stiles, who shot his jailer, and smiling Frank Stillwell, who shot almost anyone (including Morgan Earp) for money; renegade bronco Mexican, Anglo, Indian, and half-breed highwaymen and thugs—the Boot Hills of Arizona are thickly enough populated with gentlemen who came to rape her.

But these were not our heroes. Our heroes are the thousands of often forgotten solid men and women, sodbusters and cattlemen and singlejack miners, pioneer merchants and editors, housewives and senators and laborers. Our heroes came from European backgrounds of established civilization and order and rolled up their sleeves to build a great new land with fist and rope and hoe and gingham. They worked on, surrounded by toughs who were not heroes, toughs who came from the same stock of Europe, but came forward using the wilderness land and its rawness as excuses to regress to brutality and savagery, to prey on the peaceful heroes of the land who were hampered in action by conscience and scruples and chose to remain so hampered. Our heroes went on with business as usual in a most unusual world.

The bitter hardships of desert and timbered mountains and badlands, drought and blizzard, *el tigre* and the toughs red and white—these were enough for our heroes to live with. But they stayed and they fought; they did not run; and it was this kind of courage that made heroes of the people of the soil and grass and mineral lode. On the heroism of the settler Arizona built its wealth and health.

The way was shown to these settler-heroes by missionaries and mountain-man trappers. And the way was cleared of debris for the settler-heroes by soldiers and lawmen. Our heroes themselves were men and women who seldom carried, hardly ever used, firearms. But to guard their path the soldiers answered Apache arrows with Springfield Armory lead and administered the *coup de grace* with treaty from Washington; the lawmen, both licensed (like Virgil Earp) and self-appointed (like John Slaughter) were gun-handy citizens who placed their own lives in the line of fire so that the heroes might live on to build the new land's foundation of culture. These armed citizens were a part of Arizona, men like Jeff Milton, who patrolled the border from Yuma to El Paso, and like Captain Burt Mossman, who with his twelve (not yet twenty-six) Arizona Rangers tamed a territory roughly equal to the combined areas of Maine, Massachusetts, Vermont, New Hampshire, Connecticut, New Jersey, Rhode Island, Maryland, Delaware, and West Virginia.

But it must be understood that these men were not the genuine heroes of the time; they were the personification of utensils necessary to the vital infancy of a new society, but they were not representative of that society's norms. The sixgun was product, not cause, of the heroism of the times.

The heroism of our contemporaries is often concealed by the tempers of partisanship. Not so with the heroism of the past. Rather, it tends to be glamorized by the mist of time, by distance, and by the hand of the fictioneer in search of romance. I whole-heartedly acknowledge my own share of guilt in this respect. The facts of history I cheerfully warp in order to make possible the telling of a story according to thematic scheme.

The bare bones of the story here told are bound without possibility of dispute in the pages of Arizona's live history. In my home city lives a lady whose grandmother enjoyed recalling a handful of Easterners who were reunited almost accidentally in an Arizona town. The grandmother married one of them—I call him Eric Stratemeier, which is close enough to his true name. The town's marshal was a man whose skill and power broadcast the legend of his feats the length of the territory—this man has become Morgan McClintock but he could as well be Virgil Earp or Fred White or Bill Breakenridge. And the cast, with a few necessary exceptions, has come from life as remembered by a grandmother and retold to me by her granddaughter.

To the granddaughters and grandsons of Arizona this book is dedicated.

Brian Garfield
Tuscon, May, 1960

PROLOGUE

Vicksburg, June 1863. Siege guns spoke in harsh signals, and Grant's blue-clad troops sat deafened beside the trenches while cannon shells and Minie balls shot through every standing wall in the city. Dismal rain fell from slate clouds to soak thousands of troopers, each of them weary of death and weary of fighting.

All but two.

The hills above Chickasaw Bluffs, behind the siege lines, enjoyed a temporary peace born of the stalemate below. The soldier, a young brevet colonel under Sherman, stood among the trees with wet, steamy odors lying heavy against him. A Hall breech-loading carbine lay in the crook of his elbow; droplets hung suspended from the brim of his stained campaign hat; and the enclosing forest exhaled a clammy mist to make his eyes narrow and his palms slippery.

The green slope was steep and covered with small groves of timber spottily clumped. Some distance to his left, a groined creekbed cut into the high slope. Straight before him the bluff rose a few hundred feet farther, standing high against the unbroken clouds, and ending abruptly, he knew, in a plunge to the Yazoo at its juncture with the Mississippi. And to his right a ridge poked out of the slope to form a saddle running back to another bluff a mile behind him.

The colonel stood a few yards back in the trees to consider the terrain and debate his choices. If he advanced upslope, he might pass Warren Rachal's position; and yet if he climbed the flanking saddle, it could give Rachal a chance to swing down and get completely out of the area. But that wouldn't do; he had chased Rachal too long and too far to let him by now.

A sudden movement arrested him, about two hundred yards off to his right on the saddle. He searched that region with narrowed inspection, but the motion was not repeated.

1

But he had his hint. He started walking, covering ground as quickly as he could without exposing himself. Timber grew thicker on the saddle, with the uplifted root systems of occasional fallen trees lying fan-shaped on the ground. He thus lost sight of Rachal's position, but kept it in mind as he climbed. The only sounds were his own small echoes, the hum of wind, and an occasional spatter of rain in puddled water, and the steady conversations of the siege guns to the southwest.

Time slowed, and within him the anxiety grew that somewhere up there Rachal's musket lay sighted hard on him. When he crossed a small clearing, he grunted and spoke aloud: "Don't get spooky."

Never ceasing to sweep the shadows ahead, he saw no more than the quiet close-ranked willows stretching into foggy obscurity. The silence of the area seemed more intense; and then, straight up the slope, a crow called out of a high tree with a loud, squawking din. Something had flushed that crow. He had been looking elsewhere. Now he wheeled, and his eyes touched something that dropped behind a little roll of land.

A sudden shot drove dirt high around his calves. He spun behind a tree. Crackling echoes rebounded; the young man murmured, "You're shaky, Warren. You were a better shot than that."

Up ahead he caught a sudden glimpse of blue. Rachal jumped for the cover of a deadfall and went over the downed tree in a flat dive; the young colonel's slug winged thinly over his head.

The young man kept his gaze tight on that log while he slid a fresh paper cartridge into the carbine. After a moment he moved. He had a risky few seconds running out from the tree toward Rachal's position. Drawing no fire yet, he hauled up behind a closer willow, and with recklessness urging him, ran forward again. He covered the last ten feet on hands and knees and rolled tightly against the log. He heard Rachal's apprehensive voice:

"Stratemeier!"

"That's right. That's right, Warren." He touched his ear to the wood and heard the scrape of Rachal's body moving on the other side of the log.

Lying as it was, the tree was thick enough to cover him when he crouched on his knees. Thirty feet away at the base of the trunk, the roots held a great ball of caked dirt. Stratemeier listened to the steady movement of Rachal's body making for the far end where the upended roots towered. Stratemeier moved, paralleling Rachal's course forward until the roots stopped him.

He heard Rachal jump into the pit beyond the root fan. Dirt rattled. Stratemeier went over the log in a low jump and cut a quick circle around the root ball, seeing his target at the same instant Rachal saw him.

"Damn you, Stratemeier!" Rachal stood flat-footed in the hole with his narrow shoulders pulled together. The twin white bars of a union captain hung on tattered epaulets. Stratemeier watched with detached hatred while Rachal raised his musket.

Stratemeier pulled the carbine's trigger.

The slug rocked Rachal's shoulders. He took a single step back, opened his mouth, and dropped.

Stratemeier jumped into the pit. The dying man's eyes winked at him dismally. "You damned bloodhound. Two years—"

Stratemeier said nothing. Rachal coughed; dark blood welled up at his mouth corner and spilled over on his chin; he said hoarsely, "I never touched her."

Rachal's head rocked back; he was dead.

CHAPTER ONE

Two days of hard travel, from the bend of the Gila to Oak Creek, brought Naco through a barren mountain notch to the edge of the Rio Gallinas, just below the Mogollon Rim. The river seemed gentle enough to be forded. Naco gave the opposite bank a brief study, then raked his pinto with both bare heels and sent it into the water.

The pinto dipped under with its first plunge and bobbed up struggling, then humped forward and struck bottom quickly. Slack water beyond made easy wading, and the pinto heaved ashore.

The Indian swung a smooth brown leg over the pony's withers and dropped to the ground. He dipped his head in the river, ran wet fingers through his long black hair, and bent down again to drag in a long drink of the cool water, then stepped up on a rock to survey the uplands to the northwest. Here in the unprotected open, the wind hit him fully and wickedly. It was in that instant that a light gust of air telegraphed to him the warning of hoofs scuffing the broken rocks above.

Three hundred miles to the south, Geronimo was still plaguing the Fifth Cavalry. Chiricahua Apaches were unpopular throughout the Territory, and Naco, knowing this well, reached his pinto in two long strides and gigged it up into the rocks. He dismounted in an aspen grove and stood by the pony, holding its nose while he tried to catch some further sound of travel. Presently, the clang of shod hoofs hit his ears and a rider came along the narrow strait of land between Naco and the river bank.

The horseman's hat shaded his features. Naco kept the pinto quiet while he watched the man dismount, water his horse, hold his own head under the surface long enough to cool off, and come up to sit back on his heels. Annoyed by the delay, Naco settled back to wait out the white man. The wind had died down, and now air breathed wearily across the plain. Over the northern mountains Naco could see the shadow streaks of rain. Spring's temporary heat was deceptive in the high country; here, temperatures could drop sixty degrees in twelve hours. Naco's glance returned to the horseman below, now making a short noon camp under the shade of a cottonwood.

A sudden movement sent Naco's hand reaching for his knife, but the white man was only rising, apparently by impulse, to observe the horizons. He went to his horse, loosened the cinches, and let the saddled dun drift to graze while he crouched in the cottonwood's shadow, his hat low over his eyes. After a while Naco saw him lean back and let his long legs stretch before him.

It was when the white man tilted his hat back that Naco's lips formed a word: "Stratemeier." His temples furrowed with interest. From a ghostly past, Naco recognized the wide, creased lips, the heavy nose, the deep-set eyes surrounded by crow's-feet. Even in solitude Stratemeier's expression remained as it always had been, enigmatic, guarded, slightly angry.

Impatience crowded Naco, but he could not risk rousing the white man. He waited in the aspens until the sun slowly came around to warm his back. Finally Stratemeier sat upright and looked for his horse. It had wandered a few yards downstream. When the white man had tightened the cinches, he let the horse have one last drink, stepped into the saddle, and turned away from the river. He was striking out northwestward across the hills.

Naco let him get well beyond hearing, then mounted the pinto and traveled straight west into the sun, his dark eyes closely lidded against the brightness. He penetrated a single cool green grove fed by a spring and reentered the barren rock country, swinging northwest now, paralleling Stratemeier's direction of travel. Ahead of him the mountains rose, a long line of timbered slopes extending to the valley of the Ash River.

He crossed a Hualpai field sparsely settled with rangy sheep, threaded a meadow of daisies, splashed across a creek bend, and entered an upward winding pass. Red and yellow limestone walls closed in on both flanks; the sky narrowed; and suddenly the temperature dropped sharply.

It took Naco the rest of the day to achieve the heights, but he was sure that by this route he was well ahead of

Stratemeier. The sun was setting when he topped the crest overlooking War Pass.

The town lay in the spreading flat of a rugged gorge, its sprawling, crooked alleys climbing both steep sides of the canyon. At the head of the gulch a tidings slope dropped from the mouth of the Cash Box mine. Naco surveyed the town by habitual caution. A few scattered windows winked—lamps coming on inside—and a group of riders breasted the canyon mouth and drummed up the curling main street to rein in before the largest building in War Pass: Boone Shields' saloon.

Before any of the horsemen had dismounted, a massive shape strode out onto the sagging porch. Boone Shields stood with his arms akimbo and immediately launched into a speech. Afterward, he backed inside the building and the group of horsemen wheeled down the street into the stable.

Naco backed the pinto off the crest and rode back into the pines. He found the trail descending by the tidings slope and entered War Pass that way, to swing the pinto around behind the row of buildings and ride slowly down to the back of the saloon. He left the pinto ground-hitched and circled the building, then rose softly to the porch and stood outside the batwing doors looking in.

A keg-and-plank bar extended across the width of the room, and chairs and tables stood grouped around a central potbellied stove. Boone Shields was alone in the room, standing by a flickering lamp, filling a whisky glass. The man was a grotesque figure, tall and square, with bowed arms longer than his legs. His head was bullet-round, squashed into mallet shoulders without benefit of neck. Shields was black and burly and had a look of intense brutality.

Just now he stood profile to the door and, without turning, spoke mildly: "Don't stand out in the cold, Naco. Come on in."

"What the hell?" Naco thrust the batwings aside and strode into the saloon. "You should have been a Chiricahua, Boone."

"I'm a better Indian than you are, Naco, and don't you forget it."

"Maybe," Naco said. He found a glass behind the bar and helped himself to a drink out of Shields' bottle. "Ever hear of Eric Stratemeier, Boone?"

"Stratemeier." Shields spoke the word slowly, his eyebrows low with thought. "That's the fellow that just bought Hatchet."

Interest turned Naco's broad face. "Did he, now?"

"What about him?"

Naco walked to the bar and propped his elbows behind him on the plank. "I used to be trail scout for him. In Texas, maybe ten—twelve years ago."

"And?"

"He's tough," Naco said. "Watch him."

"I watch everybody, this bein' the kind of world it is." Naco padded across the room to refill his glass, and Boone's ragged voice cut into the silence.

"Why'd you mention Stratemeier?"

"Saw him this afternoon on the trail. Seemed to be on his way up here."

"What for?"

"Probably on his way to Antelope if he's the new owner of Hatchet."

"I guess," Boone agreed, building a cigarette. "Tell me about this Stratemeier."

"Told you. He's tough."

"What else?"

"Beats the hell out of me. I never spent so much time working for a man and learned so damn little about what went on inside him. He's fast and he's tough and there ain't a soft bone in him."

"Anybody can get a pleat put in his skull," Boone observed. He lit the sagging cigarette.

"He's no fool," Naco said. "When I worked for him, he was collecting mavericks out of the brush country and trailing them to Kansas. He was one of the first men to get into that business, and I'd guess he made a pretty pile of money out of it, mostly because he was tough enough not to let anybody monkey with him. I went on two drives with him, and he didn't lose over forty head from both of them."

Boone's steady eyes probed Naco's; then a smile rose to his lips. He said, "Naco, you're scared of him."

"No," Naco said. "But I know what he can do."

Boone nodded, and Naco started toward the bottle again. But then his mind changed abruptly and he swung toward the front door. Stratemeier was about to arrive.

He stepped onto the porch and heard the batwings flap

lazily behind, squalling on unoiled hinges. Sight of Stratemeier this afternoon had disturbed Naco's plans and disturbed him more than he would admit. He was convinced he should investigate Stratemeier's coming.

At eight o'clock the moon rose, with the April sky beginning to cloud up. Naco still stood on the saloon porch, looking at the sagging town, weathered into the common tangray of the land. The grade behind the trail entrance to the southeast rose slope after slope, owning no level point until it reached the highest peaks over a thousand feet above. The land swung upward in this manner in all directions from Boone Shields' canyon-bottom town.

Naco's glance rose to the distant cliffs, and he squinted. A spire of dust was pluming up there, swelling toward him. In a moment he turned his head and spoke over his shoulder: "Rider coming. Probably Stratemeier. Watch him close."

"Sure," Shields said, grinning.

The advancing traveler appeared in time over the last rise and slowly emerged from his own dust cloud. When he drew closer, Naco again recognized the man out of his past.

Without speaking, the rider drew rein before the saloon. His eyelids lifted, showed a streak of expression, and dropped. A small, tight smile curved his lips. If he was surprised to see Naco, he did not show it.

Finally he spoke: "I'm looking for Boone Shields."

"You've found him," Shields' voice thundered out of his massive chest.

"My name is Stratemeier." The horseman glanced at Naco. "But I expect you already know that."

Boone turned and reached for the doors. "Come on in."

Without speaking further, Boone entered the saloon. The Indian remained on the porch, hesitant; and Stratemeier said, "Go ahead, Naco."

Naco nodded slowly, swung inside, and placed himself by the bar. He turned to face Stratemeier's entrance. Boone was standing to his left, farther down the bar, pouring a drink, but when Stratemeier pushed inside, Boone's hand dropped from the bottle and touched the sheathed knife at his waist. He watched Stratemeier cruise across the room and settle his tall frame in a battered pine chair.

Shields' hand finally left his knife. He filled a fresh glass, crossed the room and slid the glass across the table to

Stratemeier. "You're the one just bought up most of the Antelope range."

"If Hatchet's most of it."

Naco watched the big newcomer carefully. The man was listening for the run of Shields' voice, as though trying to catch some hint of the fat man's disposition. Boone was saying: "You're smart, coming to me first."

"I like to know who I'm going to have to fight."

Boone's eyes flickered when they touched Stratemeier's, but then a small smile lifted his heavy cheeks and he nodded.

Stratemeier leaned forward to take a sip of the whisky. "I never walk into a new house with my eyes closed, friend. This ghost town of yours is hideout and headquarters for half the toughs in Arizona." His glance touched Naco. "And I'm not surprised to find you here."

Naco's brows rose. "Why?"

"Wolves like to run with the pack," Stratemeier said.

Boone settled back in his chair and said, "Make your point."

"The first thing I'll do when I move on Hatchet is tally the herd," Stratemeier said. "After that, if I ever lose a single cow, I'll bring my crew up here and burn you out."

"Strong talk," Shields murmured, and chuckled. "You'd have a hard time pushing me around, with a crew of a half-dozen saddle-sore Mexicans and a secondhand cowboy for a foreman." Stratemeier's eyebrows lifted, and Boone spoke again: "If I let a new man walk into my house, I keep my eyes open, too. You see?"

"The warning stands," Stratemeier said. "I carry a gun, and I've used it before on cow thieves. Keep your boys on a short picket."

Stratemeier stood and swung toward the door. His eyes held Naco's for a moment, unblinking. Naco turned to look at Boone.

"Hold it," Shields said. When Stratemeier faced him, Boone looked up, not aroused. "I run this town, and the hills around here. But the Antelope country's out of my bailiwick. Whether my boys bother your cows or not will depend strictly on how tough you are, bucko."

Stratemeier's small smile was his only answer; he disappeared through the batwings.

"You'd hate to find out how tough he is," said Naco.

"Hogwash," Boone said. "No one man's big enough to fool with Boone Shields."

"How you figure that?"

"Arithmetic," Boone said shortly.

"Only takes one bullet, Boone."

"But that's the last time he'll get close enough to have the chance at me. Listen, ride down the trail and head him off."

Naco shook his head. "Not me."

"You're scared."

"Call it superstition," Naco said. "I had a run-in with him once—that's why I quit him. And one time was enough for this *nino*."

Boone's big shape rose from the chair and moved to the batwings.

"Naco, you do what I told you. Get a rifle and go down after him."

Naco stood away from the bar. "Now who's scared, you or me?"

Boone whirled. "What in hell did I hire you for? Move!"

"This ain't going to sit well," Naco said quietly.

Boone snorted. "On the run, fella."

Naco considered his feet. "Get me a rifle, dammit."

Naco swung the pinto around roughly and swept away from the saloon. A mile north of War Pass, he turned off the track and rode steadily downslope through the forest for a quarter of an hour, then crossed a clearing. When he entered the timber on the other side, he pulled the pony down to a walk and rode leisurely across a narrow plateau until the aspens and junipers began to thin, giving way to bunched pinon brush. He dismounted and pulled the rifle off the horse.

He punched the gate on the frame side to check the rifle's loads. The rim of a .45-70 cartridge stared back at him. He levered it into the chamber and let the hammer back down to halfcock. He ground-hitched the pinto and walked through the brush until he arrived by a boulder sitting shoulder-high on the rim of a steep drop. Thirty yards below, a trail ran through, concealed only at wide intervals by snow-speckled rocks and scattered trees. Naco sat crosslegged beside a rock and built a cigarette. He allowed himself the risk of lighting a match.

After twenty minutes Naco heard the first sound of hoofs tapping the ground, far up around the southern bend in the trail below. He rose and took his rifle back behind the boulder. He eared the rifle's hammer back to full cock and peered at the bend in the trail.

But no further sound came from down there. A nerve in Naco's lip twitched. He swung the rifle's snout toward the trail.

Dust drove up around his feet, and the sharp crack of a rifle whipped down along the air from higher up. Naco whirled. A wink of flame drew his eyes upward, and a second bullet *whanged* off the boulder.

Naco pulled the trigger once, leaped into the brush, and ran for the pinto. He yanked the pony's head around, and made for the cover of an aspen grove while the rifle resumed, talking insistently from the head of a little cut along the ridge above. Bent low over the pony, he swept into the aspens and kept going south. The rifle quit sounding, and Naco gigged the pinto out of the trees and trotted for home, cursing the night.

"He's not that bad a shot," Naco said to his pony after a while. "It was a warning. Wonder what Boone'll say?"

CHAPTER TWO

Stratemeier slid his rifle into its scabbard, mounted, and rode down the back of the ridge to the main trail. There was a bite in the night's air and he unstrapped his frock coat from the saddle cantle and slid into it, and found a pair of calfskin gloves for his hands. Small flakes of snow came riding down, and he bound his hat around his ears with a neckerchief, bowed his head, and pressed downward toward Antelope and Hatchet ranch, still many miles ahead. Up north the height and breadth of the jagged clouds told of a tremendous wind rushing on.

When the first touch of the wind came, it startled the horse and put it into a disturbed trot; and as the churning force increased, Stratemeier heard the roar of the norther in its full fury. Then the pressure of it seized him. Great fists battered him, and the thrust of the wind made him angle the horse sharply to stay on the road.

He kicked his numbing legs out in the stirrups and roweled the horse, but when the trail turned north into the storm, the animal stopped altogether. It stood stiffly braced against the strength of the air. Stratemeier took the reins and climbed down.

Ahead, a glimmer showed through the storm. The swirling hail and snow obliterated it after one glimpse, but that was enough to change Stratemeier's course. He turned closer into the wind.

The light was brighter before him as he approached. East of the house he found a barn, and the odor of musty ages hit him hard in the face when he entered and pulled the horse in behind him. "This will do for you." He stalled the horse next to the one other animal in the building, then went out again. The wind had enough force to knock him flat against the wall. He felt his way to the corner and walked on two stiff stalks toward the light.

* * *

The woman beat the storm to the high-line cabin by minutes. She stabled her dun cowpony in the adobe barn and ran across to the cabin, light snow whipping her face. The door was locked, and she had to find a rock to knock the padlock off the hasp. She whirled inside and let the wind slam the door.

No one knew when the season's last storm would come; it usually came without warning, and encountering it far from home was one of those risks a rider of this country had to take. Memory and experience had led Kathy McCune to this Hatchet boundary cabin and drove her out of it shortly thereafter on a hunt for enough firewood to last out the storm. She made five trips, then began building a framework of logs in the corner adobe fireplace. A lantern flickering on low oil enabled her to do her job. She refilled the lantern from a can on a high shelf, set the wick, and sat down to contemplate the supplies racked around the walls.

The plank shelves held plenty of provisions. Hatchet kept its outriders well fed, and she was lucky the Hatchet foreman hadn't forgotten to stock this cabin, for the mountain grasses were strictly summer graze for Hatchet, never used until late May.

There were a number of ore charts and elevations of proposed shafts in her saddlebags, and, to busy herself, she spread them out on one of the four bunks and sat on its edge to consider them.

After a while she tired of the cold documents and began preparing a meal. It must have been close to midnight, and she resolved to sleep after dinner. Outside, the wind battered the cabin and the storm howled like an anguished animal.

A sudden increase in the volume of sound caught her as though by the shoulder and spun her around to face the door. It stood open; the outline of a big man filled the doorway.

She moved forward quickly, went around the man, and shut the door against the driving storm. "Well," she said, "hello."

When she looked at him more closely, the cold came in from outside. The man laid his glance on her like a sharp blade, motionless but ready to cut. He stepped back until his shoulder touched the door. It was then she saw that he was half numbed by his exposure to the storm. She crossed to the fire and poured some of the boiling water into a cup, handed it to him, and said, "It's not coffee, but it will have to do."

He nodded, stared into the cup and raised it to his lips. Shadows flickered across the room as he worked his stiff fingers against the buttons of his coat. He shrugged out of it and walked to the fire. Finally, his voice came droning over his shoulder: "Resurrected from the tomb. This was a piece of luck. You live here?"

"No," she said: She came past him and bent over the cooking meal. "Your boots are soaked. You'd better get out of them before they dry on your feet."

"Of course," he said, and went to a bunk to sit. While she worked Kathy studied him through edgewise glances. The man was tall and craggy; his bones were heavy, his chest and arms solid, with narrow hips and barely warped knees. He had a head of curled dark hair, shot with streaks of gray, and dark brows overhung gray-violet eyes. A single small scar broke up crow's-feet at his temples. Barefoot, the man unbuckled his heavy holster belt and crossed the cabin to hang it with his coat by the door. He came back to stand near her. His voice was rich and deeply penetrating: "It's beginning to wear off. I guess I frightened you when I came in."

"A storm like this can make an astonishing sight of any man," she said. "I wish I could offer you a better meal."

"Anything hot's welcome." He peered into the stew—she had mixed the jerky and chili into the beans—and began tramping around the room, working up circulation.

She said, "Are you sure you're all right? No numb places?"

"Not any more," he said. "But my feet need the work."

"This storm will be something to tell your grandchildren about."

He smiled shortly. "If I live to have any." His attention momentarily touched her, and she found herself wishing she were wearing something better than boots, riding slacks, and a flannel shirt covered with a dusty dungaree jacket. But then she noticed the armored expression ground into his face. It caught her suddenly by surprise, for in this land of men it was a rare man who didn't show his woman hunger. This one tempted her curiosity. She said, "Do you know where you are?"

"Roughly. This ought to be close to the southeast corner of Hatchet."

"You're on it," she told him. "This is a Hatchet camp."

His eyebrows lifted slightly. "You work for Hatchet?"

"No. I run the Lucky Roll mine. My husband left it to me. I'm Kathy McCune."

His smile was a sudden streak of white across his tan face; yet it did not break his steady reserve. "Eric Stratemeier. How do you do, Mrs. McCune."

She tilted her head over to one side. "So you're the new king."

"I wasn't aware I'd bought a crown."

"Same thing. You've bought the biggest business in the district. The only thing Hatchet doesn't own is the town of Antelope."

"And who owns Antelope?"

"The mines, mostly. You'll get along all right in town, but it won't kowtow to you the way the range people probably will. Morgan McClintock runs Antelope, and he's got a way of keeping the peace. Morg was brought in by the citizens' committee. From Yuma."

"And Abilene before that," he murmured. "I've heard of him."

"He's a fair man. Tough, but fair." She lifted the kettle from the fire. "Find a couple of tin plates—they ought to be on one of those shelves. And forks."

Small wrinkles deepened around his eyes. He swung round the room and produced from the far wall a pair of dishes. "Mrs. McCune, I question my sanity when I find a lady like you in country like this."

He had spoken with a slight drawl at that instant—the first hint of his background. *Virginia*, she thought. *Or Maryland*. He had spoken coolly, but his words made her immediately more conscious of herself. She had firm round arms and a firm round bosom, and she knew her body could create excitement in a man; yet polite reserve was all she could see in his eyes when he looked at her.

There was a crosslegged camp table beside the fireplace, and during the sparse meal, she kept her attention on him. Something in his eyes told her of a tremendous sadness, and the gallantry of his one compliment to her, and the quiet politeness of his conversation suggested a rich past. But he was a ruggedly built man with hard features and calloused hands, and it was her guess that the money to buy Hatchet had not come from inheritance. His occasional small talk during the meal revealed nothing further about him.

He waited for her to finish, then rose from the table. He spoke with soft, exact courtesy: "A fine meal. My thanks, for that and for the shelter on a night like this."

A smile touched her lips. "It's one of those proverbial nights—the kind you wouldn't turn a dog out in, you know."

Her cool humor did not seem to touch him. He crossed the room to the door in long, unhurried strides and cracked the door opened to gauge the storm. "It will have died by morning. A quick blizzard—the last storm of spring."

"Yes," she said. "There's smoked ham in the cupboard, for breakfast."

"That's fine." He stood by the closed door, staring gravely across at the mellow fire. Kathy McCune sat on the edge of a bunk and regarded him with her eyes half closed. "Do you have any tobacco?"

"Yes."

"I wonder if you'd mind rolling a cigarette for me?"

His eyebrows rose; she smiled. "It's not ladylike. This is a man's country, Mr. Stratemeier, and it so happens I enjoy the taste of tobacco."

"Of course," he muttered, and for the first time she had the satisfaction of having caught him off guard. He built a cigarette quickly and handed it to her. She looked up as he scratched a match alight with his thumbnail. She looked away to guide the cigarette to the light.

He broke the matchstick and flipped it into the fire. "Does McClintock run the valley, or just the town?"

"Both," she said, "though he's technically marshal of Antelope. We have no county officers up here—it's too far from Flagstaff."

"That's the county seat?"

"Yes."

He sat at the table. "I've bought six hundred square miles of range sight unseen. I hope you don't mind my questions."

"Not at all. Go on."

"Thank you." He built his own cigarette and waited until he had it going before he spoke again. "Is there any friction between the miners and the cattlemen?"

"Not a lot—once in a while they brawl in a saloon, but that's about the extent of it. Most of the trouble comes from higher up in the mountains—from War Pass. Boone Shields has a crew of toughs who prey on everyone. It's organized banditry. One day the people around here will get enough courage to organize and run him out. Until then, he just about controls the country—his men rob ore shipments and stages and trial herds. McClintock has been trying to stir up the citizens' committee, but they're mostly a bunch of storekeepers and saloon men." She threw her cigarette into the fire and spoke with sudden strength: "I hate all of them. They haven't the courage to fight for what's theirs!"

"Man should fight for his own," Stratemeier observed. He stood to douse the lamp, cupping his hand over it and blowing out the flame. "Time to sleep." He smoothed a bunk across the room from her and lay on it, facing the ceiling with his hands under his head and one knee up.

The fire flickered and grew low; Kathy lay back and watched shadows play fragmentarily across the pole and adobe roof. She said quietly, "It takes a good many years to make a man but only one bullet to end him. You be careful, Stratemeier."

His voice drifted across the room: "I've done no one harm."

"There will be a lot of men waiting to test your strength. They'll want to know if you can hold what you've bought."

"I'll hold it," he answered. His voice still rang melodious like a tune in her ears when she closed her eyes and let sleep come to her.

CHAPTER THREE

Rooted to her place by the table, Kathy saw him appear on the trail, spurring his horse to a canter. She went to the window and watched him swing at the base of the rise and continue northwest until he faded into the farther timber. Her heart beat small and fast; her hands gripped the sill. She pulled loose and turned back to the fire to rinse the dishes. That chore done, she shrugged into her mackinaw and opened the door to clear the stuffy air out of the place.

A rider drifted up through the brass of dawn and entered the clearing. Kathy came out of the cabin and waited while Ben Overmile advanced from the trail to loom high in the saddle. Overmile off-horsed and ducked into the house. "A bad night—a bad night. Any coffee left? I thought I might find you here—Frank Royal told me you'd ridden up this way."

"And you rode through the storm to find out if I was all right." She set the kettle back on the fire and dumped coffee into it. "Wait for that to boil. Ben, you're a crazy man."

His grin was sudden and full. "Maybe. There was another thing brought me up here—the storm drifted some Hatchet cows south. The boys are holding them down below about a mile. We didn't lose many—that's luck." He removed his hat, revealing a long head of startlingly black hair.

"Did you meet a rider on the way up just now?" Kathy asked.

"Yes. He said nothing to me. You know him?"

"Your new boss, if he decides to keep the old crew."

"That was Stratemeier? I should have known—he had a cold look." Overmile rested a hip against a chair by the table. His eyes swept the room, and his attention stopped on the wrinkled bunk Stratemeier had used. "Had company?"

"He spent the night here," she said bluntly, and kept her amusement hidden when Overmile gave her a half-aroused look.

"Stratemeier?" he said.

"That's right, Ben." She saw the hard accusation in his eyes and laughed. "He slept on that bunk, and I slept on this one. Would you have wanted me to turn him out into that blizzard?"

"Well, I guess not. Where was he headed—Hatchet or town?"

"He's gone into Antelope."

"Well, then, maybe I better get down there. Wouldn't want to lose my job by bein' late." He bowed awkwardly and spun out the door forgetting his coffee.

When Johnny Fargo awoke, he looked around and lay at ease a moment, enjoying the comfort of familiar surroundings. The room had a sharp morning chill in it and the smell of coffee and bacon strong enough to tempt his palate. The door was half shut. Someone moved around outside, making kitchen sounds, and from the street one story below came the noises of a town coming to life.

His clothes were hung over a chair. Fargo put them on, careful to straighten the collar and adjust his tie. His image in the bureau mirror was ragged and needed a shave, but his head was clear, he felt fresh and unafraid and ready for anything. In that single rush of thought he remembered the touch of Gracie's hair brushing his face, the soft sound of her meaningless whispered words.

He smiled slowly and murmured, "Let's keep it like that—always." His attention returned to his reflection above the bureau. This morning his long and softly handsome face under grass-blond hair, unsteady and restless, was content also. Sensitive lips were formed for easy smiling, and he used them for that just now as he walked into the kitchen.

Gracie stood over the stove, the back of her burnished head to him, doing work she knew well. Her hesitance to turn around, when he knew she had heard him enter, amused Fargo. He stood right behind her, close enough to touch her hair with his chin, and gripped her shoulders to turn her around. He said, "I've got a feeling—going to be a good day."

Her smile lifted plump cheeks. "Sure it will. They all are, Johnny, for you and me. Don't you think you ought to shave?"

"After breakfast," he said. Her coming down to an immediate, practical subject showed a subtle change in her from last night. He thought he knew the cause of it. He had pursued this woman for many weeks now; and last night, finally, she had been a woman wanting to please him, a woman whose spirit was all warmth and color. But now she was uncertain, not quite so sure how to treat him. She said, "I'll have to get to work soon—I should have opened the shop hours ago."

"Sure," he murmured. "Hell, those damn miners can eat somewhere else. They don't deserve your cooking, anyway." He sat down and sipped off the top of the cup of coffee.

She came away from the stove with two plates of bacon and eggs. "This is probably the best meal you've eaten in weeks. You don't eat much that doesn't come out of a bottle, do you, Johnny?"

"I stay alive," he said, and bit in.

"You know," she said quietly, "I'd like to be a lot wiser than I am. You and me—I can't find a reason that would make it fair. And if I ever do find a reason, I'll probably be lying to myself."

"The whole damned world is a lie," he said. He didn't speak more until he had cleaned his plate; then he pushed his chair back. She said, "You need a housekeeper."

"Why?"

"This place is a mess. Hire somebody to clean up after you—it's the logical thing to do."

His laugh was hollow. "Logical. From a logical point of view I've got no business being alive."

"How's that?"

"Find a logical reason why I was born. Hell, if you believe in logic, then the whole world's a fraud perpetrated on everyone in it."

"You don't really think that," she said.

"Of course not, Gracie. But you can prove or disprove anything by logic. If it's related to you and me, the relationship is too damned obscure."

She laughed. "Sometimes you get in way over your head, Johnny. You're looking at everything through a stained glass that you probably call your philosophy. But a philosophy is a belief in something—not a belief in nothing. You'll never get anywhere without believing in something."

"Who wants to get anywhere?" he asked. "I'm forty-three years old, and I'm satisfied."

She shook her head. "You've got to believe in something, Johnny."

"I believe in a man's luck. I believe in the turn of the cards and the feel of a dollar. What else is there to believe in? What do you believe in, Gracie?"

"Myself," she said. "And God. And you, Johnny."

"And me." He laughed aloud. "Of course you believe in me. Otherwise you'd never have let me—"

"I think," she said, "I'd better go now," a cool note blowing across her tone.

Fargo nodded. "I'll see you soon." He saw her to the hall and then reentered his bedroom to put an eye on the street below. He stood there until an hour before noon when he saw Eric Stratemeier enter town. Then Fargo swung for the head of the stairs.

He entered the deserted main room and went around behind the carved mahogany bar for a handful of cigars. Then he went to the front of the bar and stood with his back to it and his heel on the brass rail, his eyes on the batwings at the front. Anse Sheffield, Fargo's head bartender, came through the back door, paused at the end of the bar to tie on an apron, and began trimming the lampwicks on the walls.

Stratemeier entered the Pioneer House and let the batwings crash together behind him. Fargo watched him pause within to accustom his eyes to the dimness, watched him advance with steady strides, watched the familiar armored expression on the big man's face. And said, "Welcome to Antelope, Eric."

A slow smile, wholly without warmth, turned up the corners of Stratemeier's lips. His eyebrows lifted slightly, but otherwise he gave no sign of surprise. He did not speak. For a moment an odd light shone out of his eyes—things remembered—and then his fist came forward to grip Fargo's and he said, "Hello, Johnny. You look prosperous. Your place?"

"My place," Fargo said, with a touch of pride, as his glance studied Stratemeier. He had decided to let Stratemeier control the direction of conversation, but just now Stratemeier seemed to be willing to take his time. He accepted a schooner of beer and swept the place with a slow-moving inspection that was obviously designed to memorize the layout. As Fargo remembered him, this kind of strategy had helped Stratemeier in his quick rise to brevet colonel's commission at the age of twenty.

Milo Teague swung into the room and scuffed to the bar. Fargo answered Teague's nod and wished to God Stratemeier would say something. But he did not, yet. Anse Sheffield indifferently wiped the bar, and down at the end, Teague stood bowed over a newspaper, his lips slowly framing silent words as he read. Fargo murmured, "That's one of your neighbors, Eric. Milo Teague. Runs a little horse ranch just this side of Hatchet. He was the first settler in the valley, and he's a crochety old buzzard. Best thing to do is leave him alone."

"A man deserves at least that," Stratemeier said. "Johnny, what do you know about Bowie Cargill?"

Stratemeier was deliberately ignoring the past, Fargo saw, and he silently agreed to let sleeping dogs lie. "He homesteaded a place right east of Hatchet and north of Teague's. Nobody knows exactly how he makes a living. Rumor says he's a spy for Boone Shields, but nobody's proved a thing. You met him today?"

"He made a little war talk," Stratemeier said. "How many mines are there above here?"

"Four big ones. Clay Videen has the Contest, southeast of here. He owns the smelter up on the hill, too. Everybody else pays for using it. Ross Thompson and Miles LeVane have mines on each side of Videen."

"And Kathy McCune," Stratemeier said.

Laugh wrinkles deepened around Fargo's eyes. "You still get around, don't you?"

Stratemeier's glance fell on him, and Fargo swung to hand his empty mug to Anse Sheffield. When he had regained his composure, he said to Stratemeier, "You're the only man could ever do that to me, Eric."

Stratemeier grunted. "How much silver goes out of here in a month?"

"That depends on how many times Boone Shields lets the payroll stages in and the silver shipments out." Fargo downed half the schooner of beer. "An average might be around seventy thousand a month or maybe a little better. It's big mining and good ore—assays better than eighteen hundred dollars the ton."

"And half of it goes across your tables," Stratemeier

murmured. "You found the main chance, didn't you, Johnny?"

Fargo's flesh turned color. "I've been following camps a long time, Eric. This is my first big strike, and by now I deserve the damn thing."

"Of course," Stratemeier said softly, and turned. Morgan McClintock's big figure was outlined in the doorway. Fargo lit a cigar and rolled back indolently on his heels. The doors swung inward, and Morgan McClintock thrust himself inside, presenting a stout, powerful picture. The marshal's lips were thick and sensuous, overriden by a great hook of a nose. His gray hair was lighter in shade than Stratemeier's, but otherwise the two men made an oddly matched pair. McClintock dropped his glance on Stratemeier, and when he found a match for his cold expression in Stratemeier's own, his eyes closed to narrow angles and his hands became still. He said, "Good morning."

Fargo nodded, and Stratemeier said, "You'd be Morgan McClintock."

"You have the advantage, sir," McClintock said, and strode to the bar. Stratemeier identified himself and bought a pair of cigars from Anse Sheffield and handed one to the marshal. When Stratemeier lit a match, McClintock looked at him over the flame with hard inspection. McClintock found something of interest here; whatever it was, it pulled his lips and increased the slope of his eyelids. Fargo wondered if for the first time in his roughshod life Morgan McClintock was meeting his equal. He found himself speculating which would be deadlier—the two black-handled Colts at McClintock's hips or the single walnut-gripped Remington at Stratemeier's.

"You own Hatchet," McClintock said. "Is that right?"

"Yes."

"In that case, I suppose it is my duty, as the first town official you've met, to welcome you to Antelope. But I must add a warning to that welcome."

"Of course," Stratemeier said. "You've been hired to keep the peace in Antelope. I am subject to the law as much as anyone else."

"Exactly. I'm happy to see you understand, sir."

Stratemeier murmured, "Natural course of events, Mr. McClintock. I was once marshal of Trail City."

McClintock showed a bit of surprise. "This is not a trail

town, sir. Neither is it an open town. It has its citizens' committee and its law. At the moment, I represent both. Outside of town my jurisdiction only extends as far as I and the men behind me can force it. I'd like to advise that you'll be the object of a good deal of harassment from the toughs in the mountains. Any alliances you make to protect yourself will be tolerated by the town only so long as they don't injure the town." Having made his speech, McClintock turned and strode from the room.

Fargo looked at Stratemeier. "You'll be wise to go by his last bit of advice, Eric."

"I watch everyone," Stratemeier said.

"When were you marshal of Trail City?"

"In seventy-seven."

"But you didn't like the job."

Stratemeier shrugged. "It was profitable."

Curiosity finally bested Johnny Fargo, and he said, "Do you remember Baltimore, Eric? I wonder what became of Edith."

"I don't know," Stratemeier said shortly.

Through one of the doorways, Fargo saw a Mexican boy standing in the wind-flailed dust of the street holding the heads of a nervous team. Fargo said, "Clay Videen's in town with Mrs. Videen. He believes he owns the town. Someday someone will call him for being so damned arrogant."

"He owns the smelter?"

"And the Contest." Fargo turned to look at Stratemeier. "We used to be close, Eric. What happened? Was it Edith?"

"A man can change," Stratemeier said. "Both of us have. The little-boy games and the little-boy friendships are back on Chesapeake Bay."

"And Edith?"

Stratemeier looked at him, his face calm. "Be quiet, Johnny."

Fargo watched a tall, smiling man come through the batwings and approach them. He achieved the bar and said, "Mr. Stratemeier?"

Stratemeier nodded, and the man said, "I'm Ben Overmile."

"Hatchet's foreman," Fargo said.

"That's right." Overmile gave Fargo a quick, hostile glance. "I don't mean to offend, but a man likes to know where he stands," he said to Stratemeier.

"The Hays Company recommended you," Stratemeier said. "Let's try each other out for a while."

Overmile nodded. "Fine—fine. I'll show you out to headquarters when you're ready."

"Right now will be good," Stratemeier said. His attention touched Fargo briefly, and then he was following Overmile through the crowd.

Fargo kept his place until they had disappeared. Presently, a slight figure came up to him. Fargo said, "Want a drink?"

"Sure," said Naco. "He came through War Pass last night and laid down the law to Boone. We made a try at him, but he was too smart. Boone says you used to know him. Where's his weak point?"

Fargo laughed. The laughter started deep in his belly and burst from him to echo into the crowd. He said, "Drink up, Naco. Listen, did you ever try to find the weak point in a loaded bullet?" And still laughing, he touched Naco's thick shoulder and left the bar.

CHAPTER FOUR

A cold northern wind swept the plain. West of the Hatchet boundary, the river followed the trees for about five miles and, when the valley ended, crawled up into the tangled hills that rose and dropped from one aspen grove to another. This area was rugged, filled with dips and badlands and patternless crosshills. The road, coming off one of these hills, dropped into a shallow bowl that had once been burned out; black stumps of fire-eaten trees showed a gaunt pattern against the sunlight. Crossing this barren open, Boone Shields caught the sound of a horse and immediately dropped a hand to his gunbutt. He sat tense and watched the road to the east.

Across the burn a rider left the trees and halted. Shields recognized the man and let his own horse trot forward.

Bowie Cargill came near and paused. "'Morning, Boone."

When Cargill rounded in front of him, Shields saw the steam-wet flanks of his horse. "Marshal after you, Bowie?"

"A couple Hatchet riders. I lost them back aways."

"Wondered why you were off your range. Did they recognize you?"

Cargill chuckled. "Hell, no. I spent a lot of money buyin' this horse. Ain't nobody in this country going to catch him."

"You're a damn fool to long-loop in daylight," Shields said.

"Listen to who's talking! Besides, I was just scouting."

"What for?"

"Stratemeier's finished tallying the Hatchet herds. He's sending them back on graze. I wanted to find out where he was puttin' them."

"Well," Shields said, and thought about it. "About time he finished his tally. He's been at it close to three weeks."

"Hatchet's got a lot of cows to count."

"Sure enough." Shields gave Cargill a more careful glance. "Bowie, you remember what happened to Art

Matthews when he crossed me. Listen, you take care of your own penny-ante long-looping, and I won't bother you. But I've got my own holding pens up there, and my boys use them. If I ever catch you within fifty yards of War Pass beef, I'll hang you to the tallest tree in the Topaz hills."

"Ain't caught me yet, have you?" Cargill's voice was sleepy and insolent.

"Be sure I never do. Here's a tip. Go up on the north side and work over the corner of Hatchet. There's a lot of beef up there that Overmile never saw."

Cargill shook his head. "Overmile's a smart half-breed, Bowie. He's got Tom Brand posted up there right now."

"Tom Brand's a green kid. Scared of him, Bowie?"

"The kid's faster than he looks. He took a shot at me once."

"Hell," Shields said. A vast contempt rose in his glance, and he rode on. But then he chuckled, and put his horse into a ravine, heading southeast toward the Topaz Mountains and War Pass.

He came to the head of a little canyon, crossed the rim, and got onto a parallel ridge. The hogback was heavily timbered, and the intertwining treetops shut out the sky. His path lifted him steadily through the forest into the mountains until he at last crossed a saddle, dropped into a crosscanyon, and forded a creek running thin. He was beyond the water when a horseman advanced from the higher timber: Eric Stratemeier. Shields' hand touched his gun, but he saw that Stratemeier had spotted him and he folded both hands over his saddle horn and waited for Stratemeier to come down.

The rancher was dressed for work, in chaps and a sheepskin coat. He said, "A little out of your bailiwick, Shields."

"Maybe," Shields said. He smiled. "Fine day."

"Any day's fine if you can stand up to see it. You've got a good reason to be down here?"

"I never heard of anybody gettin' hurt minding their own business."

"That's what I'm doing," Stratemeier said mildly. "My ranch is my business. And it's closed to you and your crowd."

Shields shook his round head. "Don't hound me, Stratemeier. Listen, we'd best get one thing straight. You and I are headed for the same crossing. Most likely we'll collide."

"Make it plainer, Boone."

"That's about plain enough. I'm talkin' about powder-smoke."

Stratemeier looked at him gravely. "For a tough you do one hell of a lot of empty talking, Boone."

"Hell, I'm doing you a favor, fella. Was you a fool, I wouldn't bother with you. But you ain't a fool." Heat rose in his eyes; his jaw slid forward. "This is as clear as I'll make it, friend. There's only one man in this valley I've got to lick. That man is you. The rest of these cow nurses will wait to see what you do. That makes you the man I've got to lick sooner or later. And I will. You remember that, Mister Stratemeier."

Stratemeier was watching Shields unblinkingly. "We're one and one, Boone. If you want it, you can have it now."

Shields murmured, "You couldn't cut it, Stratemeier." He looked at Stratemeier's hand, hanging relaxed by his side; and at his eyes. And did a strange thing; he lifted his reins and turned his horse. He said, "Don't ever stray off your range, prilgrim. Don't ever walk in the wrong door."

"This is the last time you'll set foot on Hatchet without getting shot at," Stratemeier said quietly.

"We'll see," Shields said. "Watch your back."

At the end of a cool spring day Will Shawn swung his little frame onto the veranda of the Tucson Butterfield station and paused on the long-galleried porch to have a careful look at the town. The station was on Congress Street, on the fringe of the fandango district, and down the street he could see the elegant dance halls with their tired barkers before them hawking the entertainment within.

Will Shawn brushed the dust of travel from his clothes, picked up his carpetbag, went around the stagecoach, and trudged through the dusty street to the opposite board-walk. A number of cowboys came by, and the streets held a good representation of Fifth Cavalry troopers, but Will Shawn ignored all of them. His face was heavy with thought.

The hotel lobby was dim and musty. Shawn's face was a gray mask of alkali, and his lips cracked from endless dry desert winds. He waited by the hotel desk until a bald and myopic clerk made his way across the room. "I'm looking for a lady," Will Shawn said. "I'm supposed to meet her here. Miss Edith Rachal."

"She's registered here," the clerk said, "but she ain't in right now."

"I see," Shawn said, irritated. "Have you got a room?"

"Single, sir?"

"Yes, dammit. A room, man."

The clerk's eyes shot from Shawn's face to the ledger. "I've got one. Day, week, or month?"

"Day."

"One buck," the clerk said. "In advance. Want to see the room?"

"Has it got a bed?"

"That, aye, and a bureau and a mirror and a chair and a washbasin and a clothes rack and a window, and a couple of blankets and two lamps—"

"And bedbugs," Shawn said. "I'll take it." He handed a silver dollar to the clerk.

"Upstairs, next to the end on the right. Here's your key."

Shawn climbed the creaking stairs, found the room, and entered. Its only luxury was the dusty window overlooking the street. The carpetbag dropped on a chair. He removed his shirt, splashed muggy water from the tin basin into his face, and found a clean broadcloth suit in his bag. Through the window he saw the lazy traffic of horses and pedestrians along Congress Street. As Will Shawn watched the little scenes passing below, the room became close and unfriendly. He thought of his mission here—to work further havoc under the direction of a woman full of cruelty and guile—and his mind traveled back to the Baltimore of eighteen years ago.

It was February. There was a snap in the air, a light snow crusting the ground, and a breeze blowing off Chesapeake Bay. Will Shawn shivered in the chill of the dark stable and shrank back when he heard the young man's cry echoing down from the house. That must be Warren Rachal, and he must have discovered Janice Stratemeier's body. And then Shawn heard the clatter of an advancing rig. The buggy sound halted at the height of its volume, and Shawn heard the slam of the house door, then shoes scuffing the snow-spotted lawn and quick footsteps coming on into the stable.

Shawn crouched in the empty stall and peered through the slots between the splintery boards.

It was Warren Rachal, standing beside the shadow of the open stable door, utter terror freezing his face open and his hands reaching against the wall to touch a pitchfork leaning there. Shawn trembled; he remembered the girl, the way she fought him, the way he used his weight to hold her down, the way his mouth had buried itself in the hollow of her throat. He felt the terror that was this moment in the young man standing by the stable door. He remembered scuttling from the house at the sound of Rachal's approach. It must be that Rachal, afraid of being caught alone in the room with the dead woman, had fled, seeking the same hiding place.

Through the open doorway he could see the high figure advancing from the night—Eric, young Eric, ramming through the night with his fists curled tight. Eric stopped out there, beyond the doorway, and threw his head back to take a long breath. "Come on out, Warren. Take what you asked for."

And then Eric was advancing. Shawn saw him pass the doorway, saw him react to a slight sound and whirl, saw Warren Rachal bringing the pitchfork down heavily. Its end hit Stratemeier on the bicep; it was a blow that could numb a man's arm from fingertip to collar. Rachal shrieked and lunged with the pitchfork. Stratemeier rolled aside. Shawn saw him grab the fork by the tines and bring it to the floor with his weight. The fork rammed its points into the ground, and Warren came solidly against it. His breath *whooshed* out, and he bent double. Stratemeier came up from the floor with his fist swinging. He hit Warren across his lowered brow. Warren let out a roar and charged, but Eric rammed his knee into the smaller man's crotch and butted his head against Warren's jaw. Eric was fighting with desperation and cold savagery; there was nothing of the cultured college boy in him now. He danced quickly waiting for Warren to rush, and then he was chopping with his fists and jabbing until Warren's ear was hanging from his head and his face was smeared with his own blood. Warren—for Warren—was defending himself well; he must have known that if Eric got an opening he would not hesitate to kill. Eric leaped in and got one arm around

Warren. Then Warren swung a leg around behind him and pushed.

Eric tripped over the leg and fell. His head hit the wall with a hollow sock, and he slid slowly to the floor, his chest heaving and his head flopping. Shawn watched Warren stand still a moment, too punished to move; and then the young man ran from the stable. Shawn heard his pounding feet round the house, and a moment later a buggy clatter rose and slowly diminished until it was beyond hearing. Shawn moved cautiously from the stall, and when Eric did not move, he slipped from the stable and scuttled away.

Will Shawn shuddered with his eighteen-year-old memory and left the hotel room. The gathering stream of traffic carried him unresisting until he arrived at a grand parlor; he let the crowd's pressure bear him into its whisky-laden stuffiness. Past rattling roulette wheels and faces laughing emptily, he pressed to the bar, and, once there, put his back to it and surveyed the room with an eye he had trained to be suspicious. But this crowd was one easy to place and safe to forget, a cheerful lot for no reason at all, speaking loud and earnest and strong—hearty drinkers and heavy smokers and easy men and girls. Shawn turned his back to them. He downed a double shot of bourbon—it did him no good—and tried lighting up a cigarette. Lamplight glinted against his eyes, and he murmured, "That damned woman."

The man next to him swung around. "What?"

"Nothing—I'm sorry." The crowd milled around him. The man beside him left and his place was quickly filled by one of the saloon girls. "Buy me a drink?"

He shrugged and slid over far enough to make room for her. She tossed her red head. There was laughter in her eyes; she made neat work of a shot, and said, "I'm Troy. Who are you?"

"Who cares? I bought you a drink."

"And that's enough? That's all I have to know?"

"That's all."

She had a long, laughing mouth and a temper that might charm or chill. She said, "You wear that gun as if you knew how to use it."

"Maybe I do." He finished the drink and strode away, thinking intently of how often he had used that gun. He went back to the hotel and entered and stood in the middle of the lobby dragging in long breaths. "My God, My God!" he muttered. "Do I have to spend the rest of my life paying for one sin?"

Shawn went up to his room and sat, exhausted as if he had just come through a death contest. He saw in a scarred chair and tasted the contents of a tawny glass of rye. He heard Edith's steps behind him but didn't turn, and so she came around to stand before him. She glanced at the tumbler of rye, her mouth twisted. "You're so damned refreshing, Will. So cheerful."

"Oh, for God's sake, shut up." He tilted the glass to his lips, then pressed beads of sweat from his forehead.

"It's not warm today, Will."

"I can't help that."

She smiled in mock sweetness and leaned her hip against the bureau, folding her arms and tossing her head to throw back her blonde hair. "That's what I love about you, Will. Your sense of humor."

"Then why in hell don't you find another errand boy?"

"Maybe because I know you'll do exactly as I wish. The authorities in New Orleans still want a killer, and I'm the only one who knows who that killer is."

"Turn me in, dammit—be done with it."

She yawned and moved lazily away from the bureau. "I think I'll have a drink."

"You've got such fine ladylike taste, Edith. Go on, get your rotgut."

"I will," she said sweetly, "if you'll tell me where your bottle is."

"In the bureau. Here—use this glass, unless you think I've poisoned it."

"You wouldn't have the guts, Will, dear."

He only murmured, "Sure," and handed her the glass, seeing her disappointment when he refused to let her arouse him.

She poured her drink and stood by the window. For a while she neither moved nor spoke, but presently, her voice drifted across his thoughts, low and husky: "I want you to stop being the fastest gunman on the trail and start doing the job for me that's keeping you alive."

"And just what is that job, this time?"

"Eric Stratemeier."

His eyes shot up, and he gripped the edge of the chair. "You've found him."

"Yes. He's running a ranch up in the Mogollon country. A town called Antelope."

"But you still don't want me to kill him?"

"Of course not. Don't be stupid, Will. Have I spent eighteen years of my life hounding him just to let him die quickly?" She leaned forward and gestured with the glass. "We're going to ruin him, you and I, Will. He's a rich man now. We'll strip him of everything he owns and watch him crawl—and then I'll kill him."

He shook his head and reached for the glass. "You're an obsessed woman, Edith. You've wasted your whole life to get revenge on him for killing your brother. So what? Your brother was a snotty-nosed bastard, anyway."

"He was my brother, Will. You've said all that before. Let's not make the whole thing boring."

"I've been bored for eighteen years," Will Shawn said. "Bored to death."

Edith's smile was taut; her eyes penetrated into him with the shine of madness. "We have a wonderful time, don't we, Will?"

"We sure do," he said. His face was closed tight.

CHAPTER FIVE

Morgan McClintock was at his usual post, the courthouse veranda, watching his town, when Clay Videen left the stable and walked forward, cruising along the walk brushing specks of fine dust from his expertly cut Prince Albert. Videen's clothes were well enough tailored to conceal his growing paunch; but he was fat-cheeked and red-complexioned, and displayed none of the cheerfulness usually associated with heavy men. Continually perspiring, continually uncomfortable, Videen was wiping his face with a crumpled handkerchief when he paused by McClintock. "Good morning, Marshal."

McClintock inclined his head slightly. "Mr. Videen."

Videen said, "Sometime in the next week I anticipate sending twenty thousand dollars in bullion out of the smelter. I'd like to ask the favor of your accompanying the shipment as far as Prescott."

McClintock smiled gently. "My apologies, sir, but I'm only a lawman within the town limits."

"Hogwash. I don't want your star. I want your gun and your reputation."

"My job is full time. I'm sorry, Mr. Videen. There are plenty of men and plenty of guns around for hire."

"And who knows which ones to trust? Marshal, are you frightened?"

McClintock's eyes shone for an instant. "My responsibility is to the town of Antelope, not to you or your mine or your smelter."

"You want to see my men get paid, don't you, sir? That's what keeps this town alive—mine payrolls. And they don't get paid until I've received income from my operations. Bullion stored in Antelope doesn't bring income from the East, sir."

"Mr. Videen, I have turned you down. Unless you have another matter to discuss, I suggest you be about your business." McClintock waited, regarding Videen with a certain unconcealed dislike, until Videen wheeled on down the walk. His head turned lazily to follow Videen.

Men were an unsteady traffic along the street, in and out of doorways, in and out of town. One solitary figure down the street dropped off his horse and walked it into the stable's shadows. It was Naco, tough, cocky, and mean. Naco reappeared by the mouth of the stable and walked lightly across the street, where he met a second man coming out of Gracie Peters' restaurant—Johnny Fargo. The two paused together and spoke at some length, Fargo moving with restless energy, swiping the air in a gesture of impatience. There was something strange in that scene. McClintock's alert mind grew questioning. Naco finally went on down the street, and Fargo quartered across to his own Pioneer House.

Presently a handsome roan gelding trotted down the street, and its rider, Kathy McCune, dismounted directly before McClintock. She was dressed in riding trousers and a green blouse; her hair was pulled back; and her hat was lying between her shoulder blades, suspended there on its cord.

She came up on the veranda to stand by him. While she was taking off her gloves her direct dark eyes swept the street once and came to rest on his face. McClintock touched his hatbrim. "Mrs. McCune."

"Good morning, Morg. How's the marshal today?"

"So-so," he answered. His eyelids came together until shrewd lines appeared below his temples. "Something's eatin' you."

She nodded. "Why's everybody always picking on me, Morg?"

"Who did what this time?"

"It's Eric Stratemeier, and it's what he didn't do."

"Which same is?"

"He didn't come to the citizens' committee meeting last night."

"Well," McClintock said, "what's wrong with that? I wasn't there either. I was busy last night. Maybe he was, too."

"But dammit, Morg, we need him. He's the biggest single power in the valley now."

"Not if you listen to Clay Videen."

"Clay's only big until the mines play out," she said. "But

Stratemeier's got land and money and men. He'll be here for a long time."

"Maybe," McClintock said. "So what?"

"So he ought to be the one who's most interested in cleaning up this country. And the only way he can do that is to throw in with us. Maybe with his help we could get rid of Shields and all the rest of the troublemakers."

"Has he refused?"

Her shoulders settled. "No. We sent him an invitation a week ago. I went out there three times this week trying to find out if he got it, but he's never there. The only soul at Hatchet headquarters is Pablo Ruiz. The rest of them are out minding the cows. And Stratemeier's with them. God knows where."

McClintock chuckled. "I told you he was busy. Young lady, who told you to take on all this valley's woes?"

"Somebody's got to think around here," she said; and suddenly turned speculative. "I wonder what makes him keep so close to himself?"

"Who?"

"Stratemeier."

"Why, that's a good question, child, and the answer's a long one. And there's only one man in this town that knows it."

"Who's that?"

"Johnny Fargo."

Reaction opened her eyes. "Him? What would a drifter know about a man like Stratemeier?"

"Understand they used to be friends," McClintock said. Then, "Does the committee want him to join?"

"Everyone but Videen. Naturally."

"Uh-huh," he muttered. "Well, suppose I ride out this afternoon. Maybe I'll be lucky enough to find him."

"Somebody's got to. If I hadn't seen him on his way down a month ago, I'd never believe the man existed. Has he been to town at all?"

"Not since the first day he came."

She said, "Someday I'll have to ask Fargo about him," and drifted away along the walk, moving with a lazy stride, slapping one leg with her gloves.

The sun was high when McClintock put his blaze-faced black into the Hatchet's patternless yard presided over by a

U-shaped log-and-adobe house, huge and rambling. A galleried porch ran the length of the front wall, centered by a great oak door. A litter of outbuildings was scattered around the house, and a number of pole corrals stretched along from the tack shed.

No one came forward when McClintock drew up, and he off-horsed, swung up on the porch, and clacked his fist against the oak door.

His knock received no reply, and finally he went to the edge of the gallery and then down to his horse.

The horse finally brought him to a point from which he viewed a long pasture enclosing many Hatchet cattle and a half dozen or so riders. McClintock descended to the pasture bottom, threaded through the cattle, and raised a hand in a casual salute to Ben Overmile.

Hatchet's lank foreman returned the greeting and moved to place his horse by McClintock's. "Afternoon, Marshal."

"Is your boss in the neighborhood?"

Overmile jerked a thumb over his shoulder. "On the slope. Talkin' to some lady said she was an old friend of his."

"Thanks." McClintock dipped his head and reined away for the slope indicated. Soon, the figures of two riders came into view beyond an aspen grove; and as McClintock rounded the grove, the smaller of the two wheeled away and came cantering directly toward him.

She had blonde hair and a slim, firm body, and a sure ability with her horse. When she drew nearer, he could see that she was not young, but still her features were clear-cut and her direct green eyes shone. McClintock touched his hatbrim, but she pointedly ignored him, going by without slowing her horse's pace.

Puzzled, McClintock trotted up the slope to meet Stratemeier.

The rancher seemed lost in thought. His black, flat-crowned hat cut its shadow across his eyes, and for a tiny instant there was bold malice in the aroused glance he aimed at the retreating figure of the woman down below. But then his eyes touched McClintock, and the greeting he spoke was cool and unruffled: "A long way from your charges, Mr. McClintock."

"I like the country," McClintock said. "It pleases me to get out of town once in a while to ride." Now that he had found Stratemeier, there was no hurry in getting to business, and he wanted time to study this man. He said, "Don't believe I've ever seen the lady before."

"That makes your luck better than mine," Stratemeier murmured. "Something brought you to this particular spot, Marshal. Business?"

"An errand—a trifle." McClintock's head turned slowly to survey the roundabout vista. "Promised land, sir."

Stratemeier chuckled. "It may be. But as I see it, a man has the same two enemies here he has anywhere else. Nature and men. Nature, Marshal, is the better of them only because the heat goes away sometimes and the men never do."

"And the women," McClintock conjectured, and caught a sudden brightness in Stratemeier's eyes.

"The lady," said Stratemeier, "is Edith Rachal. She's staying at the Dragoon Hotel. I'd appreciate it if you'd look out for her when you can."

"She's a friend of yours, sir?"

Stratemeier smiled slightly. "Let's just say I do not wish anything to happen to her that might conceivably be blamed on me."

McClintock nodded. "I understand."

"Thank you. And the errand—the trifle that brings you here?"

"A lady's concern. Mrs. McCune has tried to find you and, I suspect, is beginning to wonder if you haven't been attacked from the Topazes or disappeared in some equally illegal way."

"I appreciate the lady's interest, but you might inform her that I'm capable of taking care of myself. Was that all?"

"There's a matter of the citizens' committee."

"And?"

"They'd like you to join them, sir. You see, we have the problem here of Boone Shields. Now, Boone is only one man, and it's possible you don't recognize him as the threat he is, but the fact is we're facing the problem of organized banditry here. Highly organized, sir. And even protected to some extent by the law. Not by me, but by the territorial law which recognizes War Pass as a separate legal community and refuses me or our committee the right to police it."

Stratemeier was studying McClintock's face. "Tell me. Why is everyone in this country so terrified by Shields?"

"Because of the great number of his allies. At any given

time that town can contain anywhere from fifteen to a hundred known outlaws—criminals at large. Some are killers, by gun or knife or club. Some are cattle thieves, some dishonest gamblers, some highwaymen, and some just errand boys. But they are tough and strong, and Boone Shields is tough enough to control them with an absolute hand."

"I see," Stratemeier said. "And what does this all have to do with me?"

"You're far from a blind man, sir. You must know by now that Ben Overmile and every man of his crew is trained in the art of fighting. It was because of this fighting ability that the Hays Company hired him to manage this ranch before they sold out to you. And it is because of this that Hatchet has been the only profit-making ranch within Boone's reach."

"Shields didn't seem to be very impressed by Ben or the crew here," Stratemeier observed. "I believe he described my defenses as a half-dozen saddle-sore Mexicans and a secondhand cowboy as foreman."

"Boone likes to talk a bigger brand of assurance than he owns. But don't let that make you underestimate him." Then McClintock said, "The committee would like the support of your crew in any defense or offense they decide to make against Shields or, for that matter, anyone who endangers the peace of the community. In return, of course, they will pledge their support to you when you may need help."

"Mr. McClintock, how often have you had to wait for a committee to make up its mind to act? If it makes a hasty decision, it is usually wrong; and if it makes a carefully considered one, it is usually too late. Thank you, no. I'll take care of my own."

McClintock nodded. "I understand. If you will not accept the committee's pledge, will you offer your support to them in time of need?"

"I can't warranty it."

"And you won't join the committee?"

"Most likely I'd cause more dissension than help."

McClintock reached up to plant his hat more firmly across his brow. "I can see there would be no point to pressing the issue, so I won't bother you with insistence, sir. I'll relay your answer to the committee."

"One other thing, Marshal. Do you know of Will Shawn?"

"Shawn? Yes. The killer."

Stratemeier nodded. "You know him by sight?"

"I saw him once in Abilene. He was quiet enough there."

"Good. Then you won't need my warning that he'll probably be making his appearance in Antelope."

McClintock frowned. "Is he under your hire?"

He watched Stratemeier's small smile split the wrinkles on dusty cheeks. "Far from it, sir. Far from it. Good afternoon."

McClintock dipped his head and swept away. While he drummed across the afternoon toward Antelope he thought of the woman Edith Rachal and the killer Shawn. In some way Stratemeier was afraid of that woman—and it was the first chink McClintock had found in his solid plate of armor. And if Stratemeier knew of Shawn's coming, and yet had not sent for him, it might mean Shawn was bringing himself to Antelope with Stratemeier as his quarry. Could the woman and the killer in some way be connected?

CHAPTER SIX

Johnny Fargo entered the Stockmen's Theatre just as Clay Videen was mounting the speaker's podium and the small gathering was becoming quiet in anticipation of the meeting's start. McClintock was posted by the wall, with an unobstructed view of the entire room. Fargo found a seat and waited while the last members of the committee filed in and sat. Kathy McCune had taken a seat well up toward the front.

Videen called the meeting to order in his own self-important way and said, "First we have a number of reports by members. We'll begin with Miles LeVane."

LeVane made his report, and Ross Thompson followed him, both men divulging information that was old knowledge to Fargo: how much they had lost in vandalized and stolen ore shipments. A young dude, representing the freighting company, got up to say his company was making every reasonable effort to halt the thefts but that the Territory's blind protection of the War Pass community made it nearly impossible to prevent losses. Kathy McCune added her sums lost to those reported to LeVane and Thompson and paused on the speaker's platform to aim a question at Morgan McClintock:

"Marshal, you mentioned that you were going to approach Mr. Stratemeier with our invitation. Did you?"

"He did."

The answer came from the entranceway, and Fargo swiveled around. Stratemeier stood just within the room, his huge body filling the doorway. People turned to look, and talk began to run high. After an interval, when the crowd had quieted, Stratemeier came down the corridor in long, unhurried strides and mounted the platform. He bowed to Kathy McCune and came forward to the edge of the stage. Fargo watched with deep interest while Stratemeier took a solid stance and began to speak.

"It has occurred to me that I have been a citizen of this

community for several weeks and have not met most of you, and I thought that tonight might be the time to introduce myself. If I have seemed to keep too much to myself, it is because I have just begun a large enterprise that has kept me constantly busy. My apologies for not having called on all of you."

Fargo allowed a small smile to touch his lips—Stratemeier was still a good politician.

He went on: "Marshal McClintock approached me with your offer and invitation a few days ago. I turned him down."

Stratemeier waited for the crowd to cease its sudden talk and then said, "I gave the question thought and had reasons for not choosing to join you at this time. If the toughs of War Pass begin to prey on me, I'll take care of those who attack me. Otherwise, I'll leave Shields alone. If you find him a constant threat, I'd suggest that instead of calling weekly meetings to discuss your problems and poking holes in the air with your fingers, you hire a private army to drive the toughs out of the country. I have seen the way the government works in this part of the country, and I believe if you wait for the Territory to solve your problem, you'll face a long wait."

Stratemeier stepped back. "Thanks very much. My apologies for the interruption." He descended from the podium, strode up the aisle, and left the room without speaking further.

When he was gone, Kathy McCune came forward. "The day may come when he finds he needs his neighbors."

"Yes," Clay Videen said, "but it may be too late. A man that won't bend usually breaks."

The meeting tonight would serve no further purposes, Fargo saw; it had degenerated into pandemonium. He got up and made his way to the door. Frank Royal, Kathy McCune's foreman, came out the door beside him and observed, "You know, I used to be a tolerant man. Then I came to Arizona."

Fargo nodded and went down the street, feeling too restless to return immediately to the saloon. He walked with strong steps back up along the bank of the river, and suddenly paused, frowning. The air seemed to hold a brittle warning. Softly running boots sounded from somewhere not too far away, circling his position. He went up Tanner's

Alley toward the lights and bustle of the street and stopped short when a stooped, indistinct figure came out of the dimness and advanced.

"Got a message for you, Fargo." Fargo recognized the voice—Syl Hollister, one of Boone's men.

Fargo said, "Why didn't he send Naco?"

"This don't concern Naco," Hollister said.

Hollister's tones were casual, but something was wrong here. Fargo started to turn his head, but it was too late. He caught a glimpse of a shadowy face, and then the man, the one behind him, came up in a rush through the alley, long arms spread to catch Fargo in a bear-lock. Fargo felt himself helplessly pinioned by the man's muscular arms. He couldn't move, and the ambusher had one foot locked around in front of Fargo's legs, to keep him from kicking out.

Fargo stood that way while Hollister continued his slow, casual advance. Hollister said, "We thought you'd get the idea a while ago. But you didn't. So I'm going to have to give you a lesson."

Fargo felt panic rising in his chest. "What the hell are you talking about, Hollister?"

"There wasn't any ore on the last wagon shipment from Videen's. Just rocks. Somebody tipped him—or somebody didn't tip us. Makes no difference which. You botched your job, bucko. And you'll learn tonight never to botch another one."

"What the hell— I can't read Videen's mind!"

"Ain't no room in this outfit for excuses, Fargo." Hollister chuckled. "This is goin' to be a pleasure. Hold him down, Art. Got him?"

"Tight as a riata," said the man holding Fargo.

"A real pleasure, fancy pants," Hollister murmured, and swung his heavy fist into Fargo's stomach.

He'd been expecting it; he'd tightened his muscles against it; but still it brought a cough up and doubled him over as far as he could bend against the hard restraint of the powerful arms hugging him. He saw Hollister's hammy fist rising again and tried to jerk his head aside. But Hollister was fast and expert. His blow caught Fargo along the side of the cheek and ripped a gash along the bone. Hollister hit him again, and again, the fist pelting him with machine-like regularity. Fargo felt awareness mercifully slip from him.

After a while, Fargo got his eyes open. He knew he was lying on the ground. He looked around—the alley was vacant—and wondered whether he had been lying there for minutes or hours. Cramping knots of pain pulled at him, and the eyes closed once more.

He awoke again in the morning and struggled home to the Pioneer House. He cut a path through the main room and said to Sheffield, "Thought I knew enough by now not to get rolled. I'm going to bed. Don't wake me up."

By Wednesday the opened sores had healed and Fargo's pains had diminished considerably, though his face was still a scabbed and ugly sight and he had to move gingerly because of what he thought must have been a cracked rib. In the afternoon Naco came by, and Fargo said, "Thompson's sending four wagons out to Flagstaff in the morning. There'll be a heavy guard—about eight men."

Naco nodded. He looked at Fargo and grinned. "Boone wants you to know he didn't tell Syl Hollister to be so damned enthusiastic about it. Hollister thinks you're a dude, and he hates dudes. He added a personal touch."

"Anything like that happens again," Fargo said, "and I'll add a personal touch to my next message to Boone—a bullet."

"You'd never touch it, dude," Naco said, still grinning, and left.

At seven o'clock, with a good crowd playing the tables and lining the bar, Fargo left the Pioneer House to have supper at Gracie's, and thereafter returned directly to the saloon. Anse Sheffield said, "You got a visitor. In the office upstairs. McClintock's with him now."

Interest lifted Fargo's eyes to the head of the stairs. Morgan McClintock came out of the office, descended the stairs quickly, and brushed angrily past the patrons. Fargo mounted the stairs, turned into the office, and paused, trying to conceal his surprise. "Hello, Will."

Will Shawn smiled. "That's all, Johnny? Hello? It's been a long time."

"Uh-huh." Fargo distantly heard the sounds rolling up from the barroom. He said, "So you've finally found him. Where's your traveling companion, Will?"

Shawn sat loosely before the desk, which supported a half-full bottle and a few glasses. The light from a smoky lamp cast a yellow glow over his face, throwing on it a wholly superficial blandness. Fargo closed the door, stepped forward, and settled into a chair.

Shawn said, "You don't look very surprised."

"When Eric came, I was surprised. But I knew sooner or later you two would be along after him. It was a question of when, not whether. Where's Edith? Didn't she come this time? Did she get tired of failing to ruin him?"

"Don't get too brash, Johnny."

"No," Fargo said. "No." He leaned forward to lift the bottle and pour a drink into a glass.

Shawn said, "You don't look too healthy."

"Walked into a door," Fargo said drily. "To what do I owe the honor of this visit?"

"Maybe just old times' sake," Shawn said.

"Don't give me that, Will. Once you were the most sensitive one of the bunch of us. Once. But not now. You know, I often wonder which of you has changed the most—you, Eric, or Edith."

"Or you," Shawn murmured.

"No, not me. I never change. I've always been a man for a quick buck and a quick woman and quick comfort. But you—you used to read poetry, Will."

"Could be I still do," Shawn said. "But I learned to read dollar signs too. And bullets."

"And you've got quick hands."

Shawn shrugged. "It's a sin to waste your talents, Johnny."

"Will, did you ever figure out why the Rachals took me in? They had two kids of their own—why raise an orphan?"

"They were bighearted. Too bad it didn't rub off on their kids."

"Uh-huh. So she's still dragging you around, trying to use you to knock Eric down. Will she ever do it?"

"I don't know, Johnny. I think so. I think this is the time and the spot. I think he'll make his fall here."

"She hates, and he's scared, and you're trapped. It's a hell of a note, Will. We started off pretty well, the six of us. But now Warren and Janice are dead—do the rest of us have to die, too?"

"Just one more," Shawn said quietly. He leaned back with his glass, gently swirling it. "How far would you go to make a pile of money?"

Fargo replied quickly, "How far would I have to go?"

"You might have to do a few unpleasant chores."

"Such as?"

"Along the order of what you're doing now for Shields. I'll get to that."

Fargo tried to conceal his alarm—how did Shawn know about that?—but Shawn saw the expression cross his face. "I've already seen Shields, Johnny, and offered him a job."

Fargo stared at him, and Shawn went on: "Obviously, I can't offer you your job on a trial basis. Either you take it, or you don't. If you take it, then you find out what it is."

"It's got to do with Eric, doesn't it? Listen, Will, there are plenty of strong backs in this country."

"Like Boone Shields and his boys? But we need a few men with more than muscles. Masters are masters, and men are men. Great plans have been ruined when men tried to be masters." Shawn studied Fargo carefully. "You've lived long enough to find out that damn few crooked men stay alive long enough to enjoy their riches. Only the smart ones."

Fargo said, "What the hell, I'll have to think about it."

"Anything worth having takes a little risk in the getting, Johnny."

Fargo shook his head. "Let me think about it. I don't know if I'll like working for Edith."

"You'll be working for me. It's now or not at all. Make up your mind."

Fargo considered it. He stood up and walked around the office and sat again. "What do you want—and what do I get out of it?"

An hour later Shawn left the room and Fargo sat in his office chair, thoughtfully frowning, remembering the smell of green meadows—a hundred memories came hard and sudden, of an age and of a place and of a tight young group of six close friends. He had a longing to return, to be what he once had been. It brought cruel pain. In that moment he hated himself for what he was and heard a voice murmur from somewhere out of that past: "You could have—" He had flung himself west after the war and come away from everything familiar. But, as always, the roads had been the wrong roads, and the same ones who condemned him as a profiteer condemned him as a gambler and as a cheat. At first, there had been hope, but now, as he faced the empty walls, he saw a world of things, and saw nothing.

When he descended to the barroom, he saw that Shawn hadn't left the building—or possibly had come back to it. The gunman stood at the near end of the bar, by the stairs; and when Fargo descended, Shawn said, "I forgot to tell you. Don't tell Shields you're working for me."

"All right. Listen, Will—go easy on McClintock. He's tough."

"When a man gets on the ground in front of me, I step on him."

"I've noticed that habit of yours," Fargo said. "But I've got a feeling it won't be too long before McClintock and the people around here decide to sweep the dirt off the streets. That includes Boone, and it'll include you and me if they find out about it."

There was heat in Shawn's eyes. "Their streets are made of dirt. Let them try."

Fargo chuckled. "Will, you've found out you're fast with a gun, and it's made you feel real big. But one day your arrogance will prove to be your blind spot. This town has a citizens' committee. It's slow, but when it moves, it'll carry a lot of weight. Watch them—they'll rise against you, sooner or later."

"Let them try," Shawn said again.

"And when they do, you'll gun the whole town down?"

"Don't despise guns, Johnny. They're not obsolete. As long as there are men, there'll be weapons. I want him to be afraid."

"I know," Fargo said. His face revealed a sudden, slight contempt. "But I don't think you'll succeed. There's not much fear left in Eric."

"And you don't like any part of it, do you? Well, Johnny, maybe I don't either. But I've got to go through with it, and you've chosen to."

Not long after Shawn had left, a big shape detached itself from the throng and came forward: Morgan McClintock. He said, "You may be making a mistake, Johnny. Shawn's as bad a one as I've met."

Fargo turned on him quickly, but then shrugged. "Who's got the right to call a man good or bad? Who dies faster, a good man or a bad one? And who has more fun?"

McClintock touched Fargo's lapel. "What fun is there in dying on the end of a noose or spending your life in jail? That's what comes to the bad ones, Johnny. That or being found out in the woods someplace, dead like a hunted antelope, miserable and full of lead."

"The good ones get hounded, too," Fargo said, thinking of Stratemeier.

"Maybe. But not so likely. Listen, I don't know what Shawn said to you, but I know his breed. The man's got a maverick stripe—he's not painted with the same brush as the rest of us. Watch him. You can't help him light a fire without getting yourself burned."

"Can't I?"

"Hell, Johnny, you're smart. Whatever you do for Shawn, you're still out in the cold. You'll profit from a man like that only so long as you're useful to him. It would be as profitless as working for Boone Shields."

Fargo put down the urge to laugh in the marshal's face, and McClintock went on: "Face up—you're no more than a small carrot in the vegetable patch."

Fargo shrugged again and pushed away through the mob. His flexible features reflected his bitterness; but then a faint flicker of humor loosened his lips.

Lee Rawls drifted close. "A good night, boss. I've cleared over two thousand for the house."

"Good. Lee, what do you do when you're caught sitting a fence?"

"Why, jump, I guess," Rawls said, and took his puzzled face back to his faro table.

Johnny Fargo nodded; he was fed up with indecision.

CHAPTER SEVEN

She wasn't sure whether he was doing it to please her or to appease the public by making one of his rare appearances; nonetheless, Kathy McCune enjoyed a certain satisfaction that he had accepted her invitation. The Saturday night dance at the Stockmen's Theatre was, aside from the saloons, almost the only recreation the valley offered its people. It formed a gathering point for everyone within miles.

Tonight, as always, the long room held a crowd. The few miners lucky enough to have their wives with them were forced to share dancing partners with dozens of single males, each freshly bathed and dressed to the hilt. As many as thirty couples danced on the floor; twice that number stood scattered along the walls and around the punch bowl; and several had gone outside away from the close heat.

Kathy paused in the doorway, touching Stratemeier's arm. Dust around the moon was a luminous ring. She smiled up at him, but his attention lay elsewhere; he was surveying the room. One large group at the room's side, by the punch-bowl table, swung to regard him and immediately fell silent. She saw a tiny smile come to his lips as he murmured, "Think they're expecting me to make another speech?" and she laughed in response.

Milo Teague was there, and she waited patiently while Stratemeier talked mutual stock problems with the old-timer. Stratemeier listened to Miles LeVane, and she was forced to listen to the mine owner's troubles too, though they were no greater than her own. Clay Videen made a ceremony of introducing his wife to Stratemeier. Morgan McClintock dropped in, said hello, and went on about his rounds.

Kathy said, "Why, that's that man Shawn." She had heard the rumors that Shawn was here to harass Stratemeier, so when she spoke, she kept careful watch on Stratemeier. His head lifted, and when his eyes found Shawn and the blonde woman accompanying him, Kathy felt a sudden tightness grip him. She watched Shawn move arrogantly through the crowd. Old Milo Teague put his flat gaze on him and whirled away without speaking. Several others drifted from the punch bowl until Stratemeier and Kathy were left standing alone. Shawn advanced with his woman.

"Good evening, Eric." It was the blonde woman who spoke.

Stratemeier made the slightest of bows. "Miss Rachal, Mr. Shawn—Mrs. McCune."

Calculated sweetness circled Edith Rachal's lips. "How do you do."

Kathy felt a sudden brittle tension. Will Shawn said, "Would you ladies excuse us?" and moved away, making his own bow and looking hard at Stratemeier, who swung along the wall and took a stance, waiting for Shawn to speak.

Kathy said, "Did you know Mr. Stratemeier before he came here, Miss Rachal?"

"I've known Eric a long time," Edith breathed. "Many years." Then, "This is quite a country you have." She stood by Kathy, arms folded over her breasts. A staccato burst of gunfire from somewhere across Antelope—a celebrating cowboy. Edith said, "The frontier still shows on this town."

"Just men," Kathy said, "proving they're alive."

"It's a strange, barbaric way they have of proving it."

"Would you change this country, Miss Rachal? I wouldn't."

"It's changing all the time. Someday this whole basin will be settled—farms and towns all along the Ash River. You can't stop progress."

Kathy said, "I don't think I'd like that. It's best the way it is." The prospect of innovation usually made Kathy uncomfortable unless it happened to be innovation of her own devising. She realized it was one of her weaknesses, but just now most of her interest was centered on Edith Rachal. What was this woman's purpose here? Was she just a companion to the gunman Shawn? She didn't look it—she looked like a woman with some dark ambition of her own.

Johnny Fargo left the Pioneer House about nine-thirty and cruised to the noisy Stockmen's Theatre. On the walk he almost bumped into Naco, but Naco gave no sign of recognition as he continued to the auditorium. Fargo paused within the door. Miles LeVane came in behind him with a jug and, seeing Fargo, paused with a smile. "Allow me to serve you one for a change, my friend."

"Thanks." Fargo watched LeVane fill a cup from his mug. "Prospering?"

"Not so you'd notice," LeVane said. "I lost another ore wagon this week. That makes four shipments in three weeks they've got. Only two of mine got through."

"One-third," Fargo observed, "is better than none."

"Sure." LeVane's face turned sour; he nodded and pushed on. Fargo leaned against the wall by the door and idly watched the movement of bodies within the close room. He thrust the taste of bitterness from his thinking and allowed little things out of the past to cross his mind—pictures and sounds, the taste of toddies in Maryland, faces of people he hadn't seen for years, a poem he had once read.

It was while his mind was still on these things that a passage opened in the crowd and through it he caught sudden sight of two women standing in conversation by the punch bowl across the room—Kathy McCune and Edith Rachal. "Well, now," he murmured. His attention focused on Edith. The gold surface of her hair was touched by glints of white light; her body, in her fashionable green ball gown, was as slim as it had always been; and her shoulders and neck were coral in the lamplight. She had not lost the ability to display her wealth of blonde hair; the cultivated curves of her body excited all his male impulses. She showed no definite expression just then—she was listening to Kathy McCune, waiting to shape her expression properly at the end of Kathy's speech. Fargo smiled. He remembered Edith well.

Then her eyes, idly roving, passed over him once and then returned to hold him. She held his glance and wordlessly challenged him to break her composure. She was a picture for his hungry attention. Despite experience, all the old impulses spoke to him; he nodded slightly and saw what he knew was a controlled break of interest in her eyes.

He moved forward through the crowd, using elbows and shoulders when he had to. He dipped his head to Kathy and put a question into his voice: "Hello, Edith?"

"Johnny. It's been many years."

"Hasn't it?" he said. He saw that, as in the past, she was

reading the excitement in him as she would read a primer—with ridiculous ease. He said, "The years have been kind to you, my dear," and wondered if she remembered how it had been with them.

She smiled; she indeed remembered. "I understand you're doing well here, Johnny." Then, to Kathy, "Johnny and I were once practically sister and brother. We were raised in the same house—by my parents."

Sister and brother, he thought. *Sure it was.* Impatience boosted fire into his eyes, to get her alone and find out the certainties of all this.

Kathy said, "It seems to be a night for renewing old ties." She was watching Will Shawn and Stratemeier.

And Edith said, "Perhaps." Her eyes held Fargo's.

He nodded very slightly. Relief washed over him; one question was answered; and he said, "It's quiet tonight. Everybody behaving themselves."

"Be glad of that," Edith said, with a little upturn at her lip corners.

"Sure enough," he said, and returned humor in his own glance. "It's been just another day." He rolled his cigar. "I guess we always stand on the edge, waiting for things to happen and half afraid they will."

"You sound jaded, Johnny," said Edith.

"Well, I guess I am." He put the cigar in his mouth and held Edith's eyes a moment longer, to be absolutely sure she knew his intentions. Then he turned quietly into the crowd, and not until he had his back to her did he allow himself the pleasure of a small anticipatory smile.

He was outside, strolling along the sidewalk, when she caught him and, without speaking, held his arm and steered him into the alley beside the theatre.

He felt like a man who was both playwright and leading man; and she was the leading lady, following her lines and cues perfectly. He congratulated himself. She said, "You're almost handsome when you smile, Johnny."

He laughed. "I appreciate your flattery." He took the cigar from his lips and ground it into the earth with his toe. "You haven't changed a trifle," he said. "Inside or out."

"How about you, Johnny? Have you changed?"

"Not ever." He looked around. No one was visible. He put his attention on her. The tight-bodiced dress revealed the contours of her body, reviving his hungers. He lifted his hands to her shoulders, and she laughed.

"Damn it, you're teasing me," he murmured, and tilted her head with his fingers curled beneath her chin. "You always liked to tease men, didn't you?" She stood passive against him. He dropped his hand to the small of her back and pulled her tight at him, and suddenly she was arching against him. He felt hot life and full desire in her lips. But then her mouth drew away and he heard the soft stir of laughter deep in her throat. "I never could understand you, Johnny. You're not half as cold as you pretend to be."

"When do I pretend to be cold, Edie?"

"Always, except alone with me." He lowered his head once more and took her kiss again. "Let's go."

Suddenly her eyes widened and her mouth dropped open, and behind him he heard the sudden smack of flesh on flesh.

He wheeled.

Will Shawn lay sprawled, a gun reversed in his fist, with Naco standing over him. A trickle of blood began to drip from the corner of Shawn's mouth. He said, "Why, you're pretty fast, Indian."

"You learn that in a hurry," Naco said, "when you're an outcast like me. Fast or dead. Next time you swing at a man, gunslammer, try it from the front." Naco seemed to recognize the question in Fargo's eyes for he said, "Mind your manners, now, Mr. Fargo." He wheeled about and turned out of the mouth of the alley.

Shawn got up on one elbow and looked up into Fargo's face. "Go on, Johnny. Go ahead and take her with you. And from then on, watch your back."

"You won't touch him, Will," Edith said. "Not ever."

The heat of anger brightened Shawn's eyes, and for a moment Fargo thought the little gunman intended to jump them both; but then Shawn's head dropped to hang from his shoulders. Edith said softly, "Come on, Johnny."

They left Shawn lying in the alley. Fargo said: "Someday he'll kill both of us."

"Not without killing himself," she said. "He knows better. If I die, the New Orleans police will receive a certain notarized letter. No, Will won't touch either one of us."

"I'm glad you're so certain of that," Fargo said drily.

* * *

Earlier, when Fargo and Edith left the theatre, Kathy followed them with squinted eyes; she remained then by the punch bowl, waiting for Stratemeier to finish with Shawn. She found herself wishing for a cigarette and looked regretfully at the crowd about her.

She glanced once more at Stratemeier. In profile he seemed even larger than he was because of the definite taper from shoulders and chest to lean hips. She felt a certain excitement in his presence and began to wonder why, after all, he had brought her tonight. He was listening calmly to Shawn, who was now speaking angrily. When Shawn finally broke away and came forward, he was smiling faintly, giving the appearance of a very mild man. His eyes were steady and shrewdly bright, and his tones were smoothly confident. "We'll see, Eric—we'll see. I'm honored to have met you, Mrs. McCune. Good evening."

She turned her head to watch him leave. For a moment he stood in the doorway, looking back. There seemed to be an immense, powerful threat in his eyes when for an instant they lay like whips against Stratemeier; and then the tall man was gone from sight.

Kathy said to Stratemeier, "I think you were born for trouble. If you're looking to avoid it, you won't succeed. Not here."

"Maybe," Stratemeier answered. "But anybody that comes after me will know I'm not a court of law. Just a man with a gun."

"That sounds like a threat. I'm still trying to figure out whether you frighten me or fascinate me."

"Probably neither," he said. "And I've never gone out of my way to avoid trouble." The band began to work a waltz, and he swung her onto the floor into whirling confusion. The craggy point of his jaw rode above her eyes.

She said, "Something's bothering you."

"The world's cracking," he said crankily, and covered his slip immediately with a smile. "I'm sorry."

"No. It's the first time you've opened up and given me a peek inside."

"You didn't see much," he observed. "If you had, you'd hate it."

"Now, how would you know that? Eric, do those people mean trouble?"

"Which ones?"

"Will Shawn and that woman."

His head rocked back, and his hard glance pierced her. He said, "I've never heard of anyone getting hurt by minding his own business."

"Well, I'm sorry, Mr. Stratemeier. But it may be I don't mind getting hurt once in a while. Still, I'm sorry if I put any saddlesores on your feelings—but this is the first time I ever really knew you had any."

"My apologies," he said. He kept his voice casual. They danced slowly, he with his head thrown back to watch her. Presently, he chuckled. "You've got a soldier's courage, lady. And I'm sorry if I've played my cards so close. I deserved the slap."

His eyelids were close; he was watching her intently. He seemed to be afraid of something developing, and she thought she knew what it was—the chemistry between them. Excitement beat in her pulse and she found herself thinking: *Maybe* . . .

CHAPTER EIGHT

At midnight Stratemeier tied his horse to the back of Kathy's buckboard and climbed to the high seat beside her.

Town fell behind, and then they were rolling at a trot along the side of the Ash. She felt a closeness in the night. She lay her hand gently on his shoulder and rested against him while the buckboard swayed and rocked down the rutted road. A rider came up from behind, loomed high in the dark, and passed, ignoring them: Naco. Naco was, she thought, a pitiless man, an Apache equally unwanted by the whites and by his own Chiricahuas, who would not tolerate one who had lived so long among the enemy.

Stratemeier said, "Years ago Naco used to work for me. I used to envy him. He goes where he wants to and does what he pleases."

"Why," she said, "you seem pretty self-sufficient to me."

"Maybe I am. Maybe. But that man's got no responsibility, no debts. Naco's his own man."

"Is he?" She looked at him thoughtfully. "He's Boone Shields' man. You're better than he is, Eric. You've got freedom, too—and something he could never have."

"What's that?"

"Strength. The strength of honesty and courage and knowledge of how to handle your power."

"Ah," he muttered. "But do I?" She felt that his little laugh was disturbed by his own uncertainties. She let herself rest more heavily against him and worked her fingers back and forth against the big muscles atop his shoulder. A secondary road came out of the hills, and Stratemeier turned left at the intersection, heading across the river bridge and up toward the Lucky Roll. At the property line he had to stop and get down and swing the wooden gate open. When he came back she turned toward him, but his glance lay northwest toward Hatchet. Moonlight on his features cast sad, craggy shadows. She touched his cheek and turned his face and abruptly crushed her lips against his mouth.

For a moment he did nothing, and then his arm came up and brought her to him. When she drew back, there was a mellowness in her voice. "I wondered what that would be like."

"Just curiosity," he said, matter-of-factly.

"Not at all," she said. "Not at all."

"There are no women on Hatchet," he said.

"Just loneliness," she retorted.

He shook his head. "No more than yours was curiosity."

"Then you believe me?"

"Shouldn't I?"

She laughed gently. She threw her head back and folded her hands in her lap. "What is it that's frightening you, Eric?" He flashed her one dark and direct glance, and then his features visibly softened. She said, "How long can you keep it bottled up?"

"Sixteen years," he said. He lay the full weight of his back against the slat of the seat and folded his arms over his chest. "When I saw them tonight—Edith and Will—it came to me that I've spent sixteen years being a damn fool. Sixteen years I've divided my time between making my fortune and running from that woman."

Her voice was a whisper: "Why?"

His head turned slightly so that his eyes could meet hers. "I killed her brother," he said. "Eighteen years ago. His death has obsessed her, and she has spent her life hunting me down, trying to strip me of whatever is mine and avenge her brother. And it may be, from her point of view, she's not so wrong after all."

"Why did you kill him?"

"Because of my sister," he said. And added, "She's dead."

"I see," she murmured. "And she has hounded you just to get vengeance for the death of that kind of man?"

"Who can say? I never knew how her mind worked. Edith is the strangest of all women."

"And you, the strangest of all men," she said. "Unless one has the key. Perhaps there's a key to Edith, too?"

"The madness of the damned," he said. "When she and her brother were still young, their parents adopted an older boy—that was Johnny Fargo. One night the parents returned home earlier than expected and found the two of them, Johnny and Edith, together. It killed Edith's father, and her mother wasted away within a year. Edith inherited a small fortune. I'd guess by now she's spent most of it trying to ruin me."

"And Will Shawn? Where does he fit?"

"Will is Edith's toy. You see, once there were six of us— Edith, Johnny, Will, Edith's brother Warren, my sister Janice, and I. We all went to school together, we lived in the same neighborhood, started in college at the same time in the same place. When the war began, Will volunteered. I never knew why. He was the mildest of all of us. I used to find him sitting on the porch in the evening, sipping toddies and reading poetry under a glassful of fireflies.

"After the war, Will was different. He'd learned to kill. He'd learned it well, and it's been with him ever since. Will lives in a dream world where Edith is the reigning queen— I think she's got blackmail evidence to keep him with her. He can't escape her, and so most of the time he makes himself think he's ruling her. In his dream world he loves to kill, but as a man Will hates killing. Someday I think it will tear him apart. Those were mad days, Kathy, when this all started, and I think it will never end."

"It will end," she said softly. "Let's go on up."

Inside the head house at Lucky Roll, packed earth floors were covered with Chimayo rugs Ross McCune had brought from Santa Fe. Log rafters supported a shake-shingle roof, and Kathy felt a certain pride in the clean efficiency of the sparse furniture of the parlor. She lifted the lamp chimney on the center table, lit the lamp, and said, "Come on in. Some coffee. It's a long ride to Hatchet."

"Not so long," Stratemeier said, but she heard him shut the door and advance.

She went to the fireplace. "Sit down. I'll have to let the fire warm and boil water."

When the fire was going nicely, she turned to face him and for an instant thought she saw a gray, moist shine in his eyes. But then he eased his big frame into the wide easy chair. She came to stand before him. He lifted his head and moved his lips as though to speak, but kept silent. He took a sack from his pocket and filled a pipe from his coat. She leaned forward, held a match to the pipe until he had it going, and flipped the match into the fireplace. Then she sat on the arm of the chair, letting her hand rest on his shoulder and her eyes on his face. His voice carried softly over the air: "It's been many, many years."

"Since what?"

"Since it's been like this."

She took the pipe from his mouth, bent, and kissed him gently. Then she straightened and replaced the pipe. "Don't ask me why I did that."

"All right," he said.

"What made you talk to me tonight? After keeping it to yourself so long?"

"Edith and Will. When I saw them tonight, I discovered what a damn fool I've been. Will doesn't frighten me. But somehow she always finds a way to get me on the run. Every time I settle down, she comes. Most of the time she doesn't do a damn thing but sit and watch me. But after a while it gets a man. You can fight when there's something to fight. But when you never know where or how or when it will come, or what it will be, your nerves fail after a while."

"So you're not as tough as you pretend," she said.

"Not with a woman like that. It's easy for a man to be tough with men."

She sat silent by him, watching him, and memories and speculations came hard and fast to crowd into her mind. Stratemeier puffed on his pipe like a thoroughly comfortable, thoroughly satisfied man. She knew this kind of man well, the man who lived for action—but who prized the little moments of inactivity like this. Her hand slid along his shoulder. She said, "I'd better put the coffee on."

His hand reached her arm. "Wait." He turned his head to face her. "You know," he began, and suddenly stopped. He was looking past her at the open doorway.

Naco stood there, his hat in his hand. He smiled gently. "My horse went lame a while back. I wonder can I swap for one of yours? I'll trade back next time I'm down this way."

Kathy frowned and stood up from the chair arm. "Why didn't you just take a horse? That's your habit, isn't it?"

Naco grinned, showing his teeth. "Ain't got much room to talk, have you, ma'am? Ain't one man enough for you?"

Stratemeier pushed up from the chair, but Naco's revolver came rolling out from under his coat with surprising speed and lay cocked in his hand.

"Just stay sittin'," Naco said. "That way, both of us'll be more comfortable."

Kathy moved a pace forward. "Take the horse and go. Who do you think you are to come into my house and wave your gun around?"

Naco gestured with his hat. He was still grinning. "Beg pardon, ma'am, but your friend here's been making a lot of threats against us hill people. Just protecting my interest, is all—I didn't mean to frighten you."

"Call it disgust," Kathy said. "You don't frighten me."

"And you won't pull that trigger," Stratemeier said. He stood up casually and turned to face Naco squarely. "Not down here in the valley where a dozen ropes will hang you before you ride a mile. Now get out of here."

Naco's grin left his gaunt cheeks. He shrugged, rolled the gun back into its scabbard, and said evenly, "Every man plays poker likes to run a bluff now and then. My apologies, ma'am." He twisted out through the door.

Stratemeier called, "No horse swap, Naco."

She heard Naco's cheerful return: "If you say so, *patron*." Then bootheels went crunching across the yard.

Kathy said, "He's scared of you. Even with a gun."

"We tangled once," Stratemeier said mildly. "Naco remembers it. Well." His troubled eyes traveled from the door to Kathy. "Maybe there's something in what he said. Maybe I shouldn't have come here. Am I trespassing on somebody's property?"

"None at all," she said. "Naco was talking about Ben Overmile. I've seen Ben once in a while."

"Maybe I shouldn't have come, then," he said again.

"That's for you to decide," she said quietly, and felt the beat of her heart against her dress.

Stratemeier's pipe had gone out. He stood by her, refilling it. She slowly moved against him and put her arms around him and felt his hands come around her back. She nuzzled the angle of his jaw.

His voice sounded faraway. "You're a strange woman. A wonderful woman."

Wonderful woman. It was a phrase Ross had used, often. She remembered him with a start and realized abruptly that finally he was gone from her heart. It had taken all these years, but finally, now, the old feeling for her dead husband had withered. She didn't know whether it was fair, and she didn't know whether it was because of this man in her arms. But when she tried to summon back the old warmth and the old heartaches and the old memories, nothing came to her but a vague recollection of calmness and content, and the hazy outline of his face.

She moved away from Stratemeier and poured coffee, then stood before him while he sipped from the steaming cup. He said, "You're a pretty woman."

She dropped her glance; he used a finger to tilt her chin up. The lamp reflected its images in his eyes. Her mouth stirred; the stillness of her face broke once more. She lifted the cup from his hands and touched her lips to the coffee and gave it back.

He put the cup on the table and went slowly to the door. He stood just outside the house, his head thrown back. She came near enough to see his face in the night. "Eric." She touched his chest. "Eric."

His eyes slowly came down to meet hers; something almost definite traveled from him to her and made her say: "What is it?"

He shook his head, and she came a bit nearer. When she spoke again, her tones were not certain. "Will you come again?"

He looked down at her; something in him—perhaps his sadness—came out to touch her. He said, "I don't know."

"Decide it yourself. Don't pay any attention to what Naco said. It meant nothing." When she swayed forward, he caught her and cut off her breath with his kiss. Then he wheeled away, but turned back for an instant before he strode off for his horse.

The sun was an hour high, the aspens to the east casting speckled shadows along the loamy ground and through the grass, when Kathy stepped outside, filled a bucket with water, and rested it on a corner of the trough. Her eyes bobbed around the yard, taking in familiar detail, showing a modest satisfaction with the house and sheds Ross had built plain, square, and with an attention to neatness and ease of maintenance. The clatter of ore cars sounded from up within the mine. She looked over the hills to the sky above Hatchet. Weariness pulled her shoulders down. She lifted a bucket and carried it into the kitchen to start the morning's chores.

When she came out again to hang the wash, the grass was sparkling in the strong sunlight. She heard a horse coming down the trail at a steady gait and went around the house and saw Ben Overmile slipping from the saddle. She smiled and went into the house. Knowing the usual course of his calls, she played his game by paying him little attention. She settled herself by the big oak table with a needle and yarn and a half-finished riding skirt.

Some kind of shadow veiled Overmile's eyes. His hands touched the table's edge. "Where's Stratemeier?"

"Why, how should I know, Ben?"

"Was he over here last night?"

"He brought me home. Ben, what right have you got to ask questions like that? Isn't he home?"

"I don't know," Overmile admitted. "Haven't been back to headquarters this morning." He looked at her with sharp observation. "You like him pretty well, don't you?"

"I like him. How's the work coming?"

"Well enough," Overmile said, without tone. In the morning's light his face was unusually long and sour. Something burned in his eyes; she saw sweat along his palms. He moved toward her, not meeting her glance.

She shook her head. "Ben, don't try to read anything into me that's not there."

His head dropped. "I need your friendship, Kathy. I've got few enough friends."

"That's not what was on your mind. Damn it, Ben, don't be adventurous."

He colored. "Listen, Kathy, Stratemeier's big and strong and wise. I just wasn't born to be that sort. Can't you see me as I am without wanting to change me?"

"Who said I wanted to change you, Ben?"

"Well, you don't want me the way I am. That's plain."

"I can't help that, Ben. Changing won't help. What's got into you?"

"I see," he said. "You know, it's ironic as hell that you'd let me kill myself before you took me seriously, but Stratemeier rides into town—"

"What the devil's wrong with you, Ben?" She realized her voice was high, but she had never before seen him act at all like this. "You listen to me, Ben Overmile, and you listen close. Eric Stratemeier brought me home last night, had one cup of coffee, and rode out. You're twenty-two years

old, and you think you can handle a crew of cowboys and a
gun and a rope. Up to now I thought you were a sweet
fellow, but that's as far as it will ever go, Ben. Look, don't
you think it would be a better idea to try and help your boss
than to envy him? You're his foreman. Shouldn't you be out
seeing what you can do, instead of coming over here to fling
jealous accusations around?"

"Maybe I should," he said. "But then maybe I don't like
mixin' in other people's grief. It's a good way to get stung by
a bee from a hive you didn't disturb yourself."

"And maybe you don't like the odds. How many guns in
War Pass, Ben?"

"Maybe I don't. Do you blame me?" He raised his eyes
for the first time to meet hers squarely. "Are you afraid of
me?" He said it suddenly. He moved across the intervening
space and clutched her, muttering: "You did this to me,"
and put savage pressure into his kiss.

When he stepped away, she said evenly, "Ben, you're not
a fool. Don't act like one."

"Damn it, you're right. But I feel trapped—it's a strange
thing, Kathy. Did you ever get caught sitting on a fence
where it was just as dangerous to fall off on either side?"

She frowned. "I don't think I quite know what you're
talking about. But maybe you should have moved more
carefully when you climbed on the fence."

"It helps a hell of a lot to cry over spilt milk," he said. He
strode the width of the room, stepped through the door,
and looked back at her. "I'm sorry, Kathy, I'm sorry. Can you
believe that?"

He had said he was trapped in something, and from the
look in his eyes she was convinced of the truth of it. She
said, "Yes."

"Thank you." His voice was humble. He turned toward
his horse and suddenly, on impulse, she went to the door
and called his name.

He turned and stopped. "Yes?"

"What did you want Eric for?"

"Nesters. Found them this morning. Camped on Cherry
Creek, on the edge of Hatchet. They claim somebody gave
'em a deed to the land and they're goin' to settle there. It's
right on one of our watering spots."

She frowned. "He's probably at the ranch. Wait a

minute—I want to go with you." A tiny suspicion was growing in Kathy's mind.

Shortly before noon, Kathy and Overmile trotted into the great Hatchet yard. Before he had dismounted, Overmile called out; and by the time she had tied up to the post by the porch, Stratemeier was through the door. Overmile said, "A bunch of sodbusters have moved on to Cherry Creek. Right on our tanks."

"What?"

"I talked to them. They claim somebody got them title to that section."

Kathy saw Stratemeier's attention swing over to her; her lips formed a question: "Edith?"

"Maybe," he said. "We'll see. Get the crew together, Ben."

They saddled under the harsh noon sun and rode south at a high gallop, raising a loud and hollow pounding across the hard-packed ground. Stratemeier said, "It would be better if you went on home, Kathy. If these homesteaders are a plant of Edith's, they might be the breed to start trouble."

"I want to go along."

He nodded and swung in the saddle. His voice lifted over the pound of hoofs: "Keep your guns in your holsters."

Overmile caught up and coughed dust out of his throat. "What's it to be?"

"We'll move them off."

"That all?"

"That's all, Ben."

Overmile grunted. "When I was with McSween in Lincoln County, we would have given them the land. To sleep in—permanently."

"No killing," Stratemeier said, and Kathy kept her stern attention on Overmile. She had never before seen this side of his nature.

The nine of them, a tight-packed bunch, rode into the homesteaders' camp at a gallop and slid to a unanimous halt, raising clouds of dust to cover the farmers.

The three farmers were hard built and weathered. Their wagon was packed with the assorted gatherings of a lifetime—plow and stove, rakes, hoes and a barrel of flour, dishes, bedrolls, and household items hanging to the highside craft. They were men with their history written in their faces—men who had left one hopeless square of land for another, always eager to travel on at the first hint of anything better.

Stratemeier spoke abruptly: "Pack up and drive out of here. This land is Hatchet. You have ten minutes."

Kathy was a bit surprised at the curtness in his voice, but she supposed he knew from experience how to best deal with people like these.

One of the three men was standing. None of them wore guns. The one on his feet was stocky and gray, wearing a square-cut spade beard that made him resemble a Biblical patriarch. His voice was low and flat, displaying little hope. "This land was given to us. We have a deed and a legal right to it."

"You can't possibly have a deed to this land," Stratemeier said. "This is a government tract, and I lease it." Then he sharpened his tones and laid his voice hard against the farmer. "You sodbusters are all the same. You poke your plow into the land and ruin it, and then when you begin to starve, you steal cows to live—and finally you move away. My business is not providing free beef to imitation farmers."

"We'll make our own way," the old man said. "I will ask for no man's help or his cattle. My sons and I live alone and bother no one."

"Friend, you miss the point. Whoever gave you that deed played a foul joke on you. It's not worth paper. This is my land, and I will not give it over to hard-scrabble drifters."

"I want no trouble," said the old man.

"Then don't ask for it. You have eight minutes. Ben, help these people load their baggage."

Ben and the six riders climbed down, picked up blankets and pots and pans, and began pitching them roughly into the high-wall wagon. Kathy heard Stratemeier's voice roughly commanding from beside her: "Careful, there. No cause to ruin that equipment. Load it carefully."

The old man, who seemed to have the only courage of the three, had stood firm throughout the procedure of packing, and now spoke stubbornly: "This is our land. We want to make a home here."

Stratemeier said, "You've been hoodwinked, my friend, and I'm sorry that it had to happen, but possibly you'll learn from this that you can't get something for nothing. You've got four minutes. Get on the wagon."

"It's our land," the old man insisted.

Ben Overmile said, "Keep lookin', sodbuster," and lifted his revolver. "Keep movin'."

Kathy watched the two sons rise to stand by the wagon. One spoke: "Come on, Pa. We don't want trouble." He looked at Stratemeier. "We're peaceable folks."

"No doubt you are," Stratemeier said. "And I don't blame this on you. You'll find a place further on. Who put you up to this?"

The old man still stood where he had been when they arrived. His voice was a monotonous drone. "I cannot tell you that, sir. And I will not leave this place. It is mine."

"Climb on the wagon, sir." Stratemeier made his voice gentle.

"I came to build a house here for me and my sons. That is still my intent." The old man crossed his arms over his chest, proud, righteous, stubborn, displaying a rare brand of courage.

Overmile casually lifted his pistol and shot into the ground by the old man's feet. Dust splashed his boots. Stratemeier said, "Ben!" The elder stood straight, not flinching, his lips clamped tightly above his beard. Overmile dropped off his horse and touched the old man's arm. "Come on. I don't want to get rough with you."

The old man spoke as a gentle breeze: "Take your hand off me, sir."

Overmile shoved, and Kathy watched the old man sprawl. Overmile's lips spread thinner. "Climb on the wagon, old fella."

By then Stratemeier was off his horse. He grabbed Overmile's shoulder and swung him roughly away; he knelt and helped the old man to his feet. "My apologies," he said.

The old man shook his head. He had made his play, and now pride would not let him back down.

Stratemeier said, "I'll help you on the wagon, sir," but the two sons came forward, took the old man, and set him on the high seat. The old man sat silent, his jaws clamped. The two sons climbed to the wagon, heads down, and drove slowly toward the river bridge. Stratemeier went to his horse and swung up quickly. "Get on your horse, Ben, and come over here."

Overmile mounted and reined his horse around. Kathy saw Stratemeier lay a heavy-lidded glance on him, cold and almost arrogant. She barely heard his words, and knew the rest of the crew could not hear: "Bucko, you're breeding a hell of a scab on your nose. Disobey me once more and you'll be looking for a new job."

"Sorry," Overmile said curtly, and wheeled his horse away. He drummed up over the hill at a gallop and spurred out of sight.

Stratemeier set out in the same direction at a slower gait. Kathy put her horse alongside and heard the six Hatchet men trotting behind. She said, "She's starting to stab at you."

"Yes. But this time it will do her no good. I'm staying here, Kathy."

"That's fine, Eric," she breathed. "That's fine."

They were crossing the meadow, threading a scattering of cattle, when Ben Overmile appeared ahead and rode down swiftly toward them. He swirled to a halt and spoke with short wind: "Juan Soto caught me on the trail. Says he was just up at the badlands edge. A bunch of riders rode down there this morning to rustle the herd. Soto and Munguia and Charley Sharpe gave them a fight. Soto got out with a busted wing. Charley and Munguia are dead."

Kathy heard his words as shocking slaps; she swung her wide glance to Stratemeier. His long jaw crept forward to make a thin line; his eyes narrowed, and he looked at her. He said, "You ride on home," then turned to the crew. "Spread out in twos and start checking the herds. If you see anybody coming and you don't like their looks, fan your tails out of there and get a crowd and go back after them. Come on, Ben."

CHAPTER NINE

Overmile followed Stratemeier at a gallop, casually inspecting the horizons—and saw a group of riders slowly advancing in shadowy file through the trees from the westward cliffs. They came forward, drifting toward the thin scatter of a few Hatchet cattle grazing near the trees. It was when they began pushing the cattle that Stratemeier lifted the rifle from his saddle boot. "They came back for more. I expect that's what they'll get." Overmile lifted his own rifle; when he looked down the barrel, one of the riding shapes loomed indistinctly before it. His shot echoed back from the hills, and then the riders were suddenly rushing away.

Stratemeier said, "Let's go."

Overmile touched his arm. "Settle down. They'll hit the War Pass trail and lose their tracks in the traffic up there. We should have ambushed them from up above. Too late now."

Stratemeier gave him a hot glance. "For a fighter you're mighty disposed to let them get away free from this one, Ben. You coming?"

Overmile shrugged; it wouldn't do to make Stratemeier suspicious. "I guess so."

They crossed the bowl at a gallop and rose into the foothills. The thieves were out of sight, but their dust still hung in the air. While they ran over the top of a hill, Overmile pointed southwest. "They're headed for Pinto Canyon."

Overmile got a last glimpse of the riders ahead, going up into the canyon with a swell and a rush, and he and Stratemeier raced across the flats and dropped into the canyon, climbed swiftly through it and came out at the topside trail, which went straight south through the timber until it dropped into a small grassy dish surrounded by rock peaks. Here the trail forked and Stratemeier pulled in, frowning. A small stream fed the grass here, and there was no dust to indicate the direction of travel. Overmile nosed around and presently called, "Over here," Stratemeier swung to join him.

Hoofs had knocked the grass down. Overmile said, "Looks like they headed east, for War Pass."

Stratemeier gave him a single sharp glance and shook his head. "A man knocks grass down toward his direction of travel. A horse does the opposite. They're going west—see the trees up there?"

"All right," Overmile conceded, and they moved out, trotting now, keeping the pace down to avoid losing the dim trail. From time to time a single set of tracks left the main trail to leave the bunch, but they stuck with the main group. They were climbing toward the peaks now, and boulders and trees were more plentiful in this heavily timbered hogback. At the edge of one clearing the remaining tracks split up, each horse going its own way. Overmile said, "We'll never get them now."

"One at a time," Stratemeier said. "We can get two of them. Pick a trail and stick on it."

"And if I lose him?"

"Go on home. I'll meet you there."

"When?"

"When I'm through up here, damn it. Get going, Ben."

"If I find him?"

"Take him alive if you can," Stratemeier muttered, his eyes on the diverging tracks. "On the run."

"Sure," Overmile muttered, and swung northeast, his head bowed as he studied the ground ahead of him. He felt the cool touch of fear, that perhaps his reluctance had been too obvious to Stratemeier; but then he settled his shoulders. "Got to get off this damned fence sometime," he muttered. He pressed steadily deeper toward the center of the range until, long after the moon had set, he had come to a point not more than five or six miles southwest of Hays Pass.

The first pale signs of day were rippling up over the eastern rock silhouettes when he started switchbacking down toward a cottonwood meadow. Darkness still protected the tiny valley, and a single patch of orange light flickering far ahead was someone's campfire. Even from here he could smell its smoke. Then he was out of the pines and into the cottonwoods. He reined down to a walk and kept within the deepest chain of timber marching toward that signal. A smart man, on the run, never stayed within the circle of light cast by his fire, and if this fire belonged to the man Overmile sought, that man might be bedded down many yards away, hoping his horse would give him sufficient warning of approaching trouble. Or he might be waiting along his own backtrail, setting a trap.

Either way Overmile would need caution. A quarter mile from the blaze he dismounted, left the dun ground-hitched, and continued through the trees on foot. He swung right and circled the fire, keeping a five-hundred-yard radius between it and himself. When he started to move in on the blaze from the north, the first peak of the fall sun appeared.

With daylight, the fire was harder to spot through the cottonwood trunks, but soon the sky became light enough to show him the rising smoke spiral. The fire sat in a small clearing. A bridled roan stood hipshot a few feet from the campfire, tied loosely to a sapling; and a roll of blankets lying by the grounded saddle looked like a sleeping man at first glance. "That would have done the trick at night," Overmile observed, turning east to get up on the ridge behind the slope. When he had achieved the ridgetop, he stood at the trees' edge. The scratch of a rolling pebble from somewhere lower on the slope warned him, and when he looked that way, he saw the brush clump wiggling where there was no wind. Overmile stepped forward, palmed his gun. "You can come on out, Arnie."

"What the hell?" The voice came from the brush, and so did the man who stepped forward warily. Overmile's revolver was in his right hand. Overmile kept his grin steady while Arnie, a rifle cradled in the crook of his arm, advanced slowly, puzzled. Arnie shifted his grip to swing the rifle cautiously toward Overmile, and Overmile lifted his revolver and held it trained on the man. "Put the rifle away, Arnie. Come on up here."

Arnie shrugged; he seemed to feel secure. He returned the rifle to the bend of his elbow and sauntered up. "What the hell are you doing up here?" he said.

"I thought we had a deal, Arnie. What were you doing with that crew cutting Hatchet cows?"

"Why don't you talk to Boone about it?"

"Maybe I won't have to," Overmile said. "What's it all about, Arnie?"

"I don't know. Boone says the deal's off and somebody's makin' it worth our while to pester Hatchet for a while."

"Did you have to kill Munguia and Charley Sharpe?"

"Wasn't none of my doin'," Arnie said. "That was Syl Hollister."

Overmile nodded. "Well, I'll see to him later. Listen, Arnie, I can't afford to let you fellows start pilfering Hatchet stock."

"I can't help that. If you live in Boone's country, you follow his orders or wind up with a bullet in your gut. Don't complain to me about it."

"No," Overmile said. "But I'll have to throw the fear of God into Boone. And I know one way to do that." His hand casually rose with the revolver. Arnie took two rapid steps back, trying to swing his rifle in line, and Overmile's pistol boomed twice.

Arnie's rifle fell. He stumbled forward, clawed at Overmile's shoulder, and fell. Overmile holstered the pistol and knelt by Arnie.

The clatter of bootheels on rock telegraphed down along the ground from higher up, and Overmile wheeled. It was Stratemeier, walking forward with long strides. Overmile covered his surprise with an expression of quick candor. Stratemeier said, "What in hell did you do that for?"

"You saw him lift the rifle."

"Yeah," Stratemeier murmured, his eyes narrow. "Who was he?"

"One of the thieves. Arnie Ward. He worked for Boone."

Stratemeier knelt to have a closer look at the dead man. "Might have gotten some answers from him."

"What you want answers for? He rustled the cattle, didn't he? He was with the bunch that gunned Munguia and Charley."

"I want to find out who put them up to this," Stratemeier said. "I've got to make sure." He brought his eyes around to rest flatly on Overmile. "You seem to know a lot more than you've told me about Boone's crowd. You've been tying up with them, haven't you?"

"I've had a few dealings with them," Overmile admitted. "I never figured it would hurt to find out as much as I could about them."

"Or maybe it's more than that," Stratemeier suggested. When his eyes met Overmile's, there was a point of flame in them. "You ran with that pack of wolves down in Lincoln County once, didn't you?"

"Sure. What of it?" Crouched on his heels, Overmile extended his hand, palm out. "Listen. This damned world will beat the guts out of you if you let it. Sure, I've made a few deals with these boys. It was for our own protection—yours and mine and Hatchet's. I've saved us a lot of stock that way. We haven't lost a third the cattle from rustling that any of the other valley outfits have."

"What kind of deals?" Stratemeier's voice was flat.

Overmile shrugged and stood up. "Simple. The boys and I keep our mouths shut about who we see crossing Hatchet range. In return for that, nobody bothers us."

"All right. I'll choose to believe you, but I'll tell you one thing: It stops right now. Anybody riding across Hatchet will have to take his chances against our guns."

Overmile shook his head. "Listen, if I can get to Boone, maybe I can talk him out of this business. God knows why he hit us yesterday. If we start shooting trespassers, our skins won't be worth a Confederate dollar."

"Grow up, Ben," Stratemeier murmured. "You've got long pants on now. You can't make deals with crooks."

"Hell, some of these boys up in the hills aren't half as crooked as the respectable bankers down in Prescott."

Stratemeier's jaw lay forward in a long, hard line. "Hatchet is closed to Boone's boys. If you ever forget that, Ben, consider yourself fired." He turned to the head of the talus slope and started picking his way down. "Maybe there's a shovel around this camp somewhere. We'll bury him."

CHAPTER TEN

Night fully blacked the land, with no moon and no stars glowing past the massed clouds, when Edith climbed the stairs of the Dragoon Hotel and entered Will Shawn's room.

Shawn lay on the faded bedspread, his booted feet crossed. He held his head in his locked fingers and twisted his neck to look at her. She tried to fathom his expression, and he said, "It will be difficult for you, my dear, but I hope you can manage to look cheerful tonight."

The glance she gave him was bored. She dropped into a chair and watched him steadily. He said, "Be pleasant, Edith. They'll appreciate it. I will, too." There was a dryness in his voice, ruthless and intolerant.

"Come down out of the clouds," she said. "I wish you'd be able to remember not to talk to me like that, Will. I don't care what your own dreams are, but don't make the mistake of trying to fit the world into them. You're not the top gun in this room. Don't order me around."

Shawn grumbled, rolled off the bed, and went to the door. Edith said, "Don't parade your gun around the saloons tonight, Will. We've got work to do."

"I'll be downstairs," he said, and went. She stood listening to his steps on the staircase, then walked to the window and opened it to allow the cold wind to sweep through the musty room. She stood in that wind, arms folded over her breasts, and her thoughts came around to Stratemeier, as they most always did. *Strange the way he keeps coming back to me. Why didn't I forget him?* She was proud that she could admit privately that she had never loved Stratemeier or any other man. Yet the memory of a man could come to hurt and haunt, and she wondered why it was that Stratemeier had to be crushed. Long ago there had been a reason for it, but that reason had been buried in the dust somewhere back along the years, and now she had the feeling that her quest for vengeance rose out of habit more than anything else. But there had to be a reason for living. *You can tell the world it's on account of Warren. But he was a no-good brother—what do you tell yourself?*

She went down to the lobby, took Shawn's elbow, and went through the town smiling. The Stockmen's Theatre was filling. The doctor, the hotel manager, Satterlee of Satterlee's Mercantile, Morgan McClintock, old Milo Teague, self-appointed Judge Conrad—the auditorium swirled with members of the citizens' committee. Edith glided forward in her lacy red gown, and Shawn strode beside her, a small but commanding figure in black broadcloth. They took a pair of seats on the stage, behind the speaker's dais, and sat watching the crowd. She saw Johnny Fargo drift in. He nodded to her and smiled coldly at Shawn—and a while later she saw the tall, blackhaired figure of Stratemeier's foreman Overmile swinging inside. She frowned. Presently, the mining contingent entered in a cluster—LeVane, Thompson, Kathy McCune, and Videen. These four mounted the stage and took their places in chairs racked on both sides of her. Clay Videen went forward and raised both thick hands, commanding silence.

"Fourth of June," Videen said. "The meeting will come to order. I'd like to announce a couple of guests with us tonight. And I think we can dispense with the customary reports of losses due to robbery and vandalism." His bull head swung to sweep the crowd and he added drily, "Losses have kept right on schedule, thanks to the efficiency of the population of War Pass."

She looked down past him and saw Naco drifting through the crowd, squat and brown. Naco was unpopular with all of them and came knowing it and allowing it to evoke his even, sadistic grin. Videen said, "Now, ladies and gentlemen, I'd like to introduce a new member of our community—Miss Edith Rachal."

Videen bowed to her and crossed the stage to take his seat. Edith rose and stood beside the dais, not on it. She knew her gown was a flattering outline for her trim, tall figure. Her smile was vague and deceptively quiet, accenting the serene self-control she liked to demonstrate. When she began to speak, it was in a well-modulated, mild tone. *The campaign will hereby begin,* she thought.

"I'm not a member of your committee—or even of your town, for that matter. It may be that because of this you don't consider I have much of a right to speak before you.

But I have brought with me tonight some documented evidence that may be helpful to you here.

"I know you've all expressed sympathy for Mr. Stratemeier, the new owner of Hatchet, since the death of two of his men and the loss of so many of his cattle and, most recently, the destruction of his headquarters by fire. Well, I'd advise that you not feel too sorry for Mr. Stratemeier. The death of the two cowboys was unfortunate, and most probably he had nothing to do with that. But it may well be that your new neighbor has been behind the other so-called misfortunes at Hatchet ranch. No, don't scoff. It does sound ridiculous—why would a man burn down his own house and steal his own cattle? Or hire it done? The answer, I think, is insurance. Hatchet ranch is insured for a great amount of money."

Edith kept rigidly careful attention on the faces massed before her. While she spoke she studied each one— McClintock, skeptical but silent; Overmile, reddening and tightening his lips in anger; Fargo, his mouth half open in surprise, as were so many others; Naco, standing by the wall with folded arms and a half-smile; and the many others, surprised and shocked and half-believing her. She went on rapidly:

"The evidence I have is in a group of collected newspaper reports. I showed them to Mr. McClintock this afternoon, and he suggested I bring it up before you. Let me read from a few."

She withdrew from her handbag a number of irregular clippings and shuffled through them, finally picking one. "This is from the Trail City *Times*, dated July 19, 1877. 'Early yesterday afternoon the Texas Palace burned to the ground. There were no injuries or deaths reported, but damages have been estimated at eighteen thousand dollars.' On down in the column it mentions that the Texas Palace was owned by two partners—Elliot Mossgrove and Eric Stratemeier.

"A later edition of the same newspaper, dated August 14, 1877, has a small article reporting that the full value of coverage, in cash, would be awarded to the co-owners of the Texas Palace by the Smoot Insurance Company.

"A third article says: 'Mr. Elliot Mossgrove disclosed yesterday that he has bought, for cash, the full interests of his partner, Eric Stratemeier, in the Texas Palace, now in the process of reconstruction.'"

Edith looked through the crowd again. "The insurance investigator could have missed something. It's too coincidental that Mr. Stratemeier should have two enterprises destroyed by fire within four years—especially when both were heavily insured. There are other reports here of different catastrophes. In 1868 the Dilton Ranch in East Texas lost a herd of thirty-nine hundred cattle in the vicinity of the Canadian River. The herd was being traildriven to Kansas. It's trail boss was Eric Stratemeier. He claimed the herd was lost because of a stampede in a thunderstorm and subsequent raids by Indians. But two months later, Eric Stratemeier arrived in Kansas at the railroad with a herd of thirty-four hundred cattle which he claimed were his. He took cash payment for the sale of them.

"In 1879 the Hard Luck Casino in Leadville burned to the ground. The insurance was claimed by the owner, who called himself Eldon Swain. The initials match Mr. Stratemeier's, and I have other reasons for believing that Eldon Swain and Eric Stratemeier are one and the same. In 1863 Mr. Stratemeier was a colonel in the Union Army. He was convicted of second-degree murder for killing a fellow Union officer and was imprisoned at Fort Leavenworth. In April, 1865, the general amnesty for all prisoners in Federal prisons somehow included him, and he was released. Two months later authorities in New Orleans arrested a man identified as Eldon Swain. He was arrested for attempted destruction of property by fire, the motive being recovery of insurance. The property was his own. Unfortunately, Mr. Swain escaped."

She paused and watched the reaction to this accumulated accusation. A murmur of excitement swept the room, rising and falling. Overmile and Fargo registered frank, shocked disbelief. The others looked as though they were mostly willing to believe her but didn't quite know what to do about it. She wanted to turn around and look at Kathy McCune, but she did not.

The dead silence that had accompanied her speech resumed. She said: "Any of you who would like to verify these clippings or read them in more detail are welcome to do so. I'm afraid I have no suggestions for action, since nothing can be proved against Mr. Stratemeier—nothing that would stand up in court, at least. And the day for lynchings is probably past. But I did want you to know these things so that you'll be able to watch what happens with open eyes and with the truth at your disposal. Thank you very much for your time."

When she turned and went back to her chair, she glanced down the row of seats at Kathy McCune, and could hardly hide her amusement. Kathy was trying not to believe it, but she wasn't succeeding too well. Edith sat down and watched Videen march up to the dais. Will Shawn leaned toward her and whispered, "Very well done, my dear. Well done indeed. This is the best you've ever presented it." She didn't allow herself to smile, and Shawn said, "When did they burn down Hatchet? I didn't know Boone had accomplished that yet."

"Last night," she murmured. "It seems odd that Overmile would be here tonight—Eric's up in the mountains with the rest of the crew. But they won't find anyone at War Pass. The place is deserted."

"Where's Boone?"

"Somewhere in the hills, hiding. He'll go home when Eric leaves the mountains, which he will. Soon, I think. He can't leave his cattle unguarded."

Shawn snorted. "And I thought I was supposed to give Boone his orders."

"You were drunk yesterday," she murmured, and looked again at Ben Overmile, who sat regarding her darkly. She thought, *Did Eric send him to watch us?*

Presently, the formality of the meeting ended, and Videen led the mine owners up the aisle and out. The crowd began to break up. Kathy McCune swept past Edith with one wicked glance and strode from the room without a greeting. Edith stood by the base of the stage and saw Ben Overmile approach the spot where Naco leaned insolently against the wall. She heard Overmile say: "Who let you in?"

"Nobody kept me out," Naco said.

"I don't suppose you had anything to do with our bonfire," Overmile said.

"I was in town last night. All night."

"Of course," Overmile said.

Naco stood away from the wall, ruffled. "Look here, Overmile, quit riding me. Why is it you big fellows always think a two-bit cowboy like me's fair game?"

"That so?" Overmile said. "Funny—I always figured it was the other way around." He wheeled down the wall and went out the side door.

Edith said to Shawn, "I thought you told me Overmile was working with Shields."

Shawn took her arm and guided her to the street, speaking softly. "Overmile's a funny one—an old breed. He hasn't got many scruples, but he's got a great loyalty to his hire. He made a deal with Boone because it benefited Hatchet. But now Boone's gone against Hatchet and Overmile's done with him."

"I see," she said, "you've become quite a legend, Will. I watched those men look at you tonight. They're afraid of you, but most of them are waiting for the day they can see a man like you humble. Some of them are hoping McClintock will do it. Be easy with him—you can't afford to provoke him."

Shawn's eyelids fluttered. He said, "You've got a way of handling anyone. But don't be too damned sure of yourself, lady."

"Don't be ambitious, Will. Only one of us can be top dog. I'm it."

He turned to face her, deep-eyed and dry-lipped. "What happens when you run him out of here? The same thing all over again?"

"No," she said. "There won't be another time. This time we'll crush him right here before he has a chance to run."

"Aagh," he said. "You've said that before."

"Have I?"

"Edith, you're a damn small and pretty woman, you know it? When you get old, you'll sit in a parlor and serve tea to other old hags while you all wallow in malicious gossip. The only things you've got are good looks and hate, and neither one of them will last. You lost the only man you ever really wanted—Stratemeier—because you wouldn't give him any faith or love in return. And on top of it all, you're a tramp. You ran around with Fargo when you were both in school. You ran around with me after he left, when you were supposed to be Eric's. I'll bet there are dozens of men across the country—"

She said, "Shut up, Will," then fell silent. How long could she make excuses for herself? Suddenly Edith realized that even though she must fight him constantly, she must at all costs keep Stratemeier alive.

Johnny Fargo entered Shawn's room, closed the door, and leaned his back to it. "What she said—was it true?"

Shawn looked up sleepily from his bed. He had not undressed. His smile was quick and deadly. "You'd like to think so, wouldn't you, Johnny? It would make you feel a little less guilty for lighting that match last night."

"Was it true, damn it?"

Shawn shook his head. "Hell, no. Some of it was, but not the whole thing."

Fargo was insistent. "How much?"

Shawn let his shoulders rise and drop. "All right. There was a man named Eldon Swain. He died a few years ago, of strangulation. A rope. He was the one they arrested in New Orleans and the one who had his saloon burn down in Leadville. What she said about the Texas Palace was true, only I was the one who burned it. We were trying to pin an insurance-claim fire on him, but it didn't work—the evidence got buried somehow. It was Edith's crew that stole that herd on the Canadian, not Indians. He got the other herd from a partner, Elliot Mossgrove, and drove it to Kansas later the same year. I guess he and Mossgrove split the profit, but they did own the cattle. Happy now, Johnny?"

Fargo grunted and swung out the door. He returned directly to the Pioneer House, to his rooms. He lay on the sofa and stared at the ceiling.

In the morning he blinked and rose stiffly from the sofa, went into his bedroom, changed into fresh clothes, and descended to the street. He looked sourly at the town.

Clay Videen strolled heavily by, gave him one haughty glance, and disappeared into the Dragoon Hotel. Naco appeared on his horse at the stable mouth, entered the street, and cantered past, whipping one meaningful glance at Fargo and then riding directly out of town. Fargo felt a little chill. That one brief glimpse of Naco's eyes crystallized Fargo's plan; his fists tightened with bitter resolution. He turned with an abrupt snap of his shoulders and strode rapidly across the diagonal of the street to Gracie's. When he entered, he stood a moment hesitant within the door. Gracie was alone behind the kitchen counter. She nodded without exuberance and came slowly forward. "You're up early, Johnny."

"Not early enough," he said. "Gracie, I'm thinking of leaving this country. I'd like you to come with me."

"Where?"

He shrugged. "Who cares? Over the hills—anywhere. I've got to start new. Back East, maybe."

Her careful glance widened and held him; their eyes locked while she weighed his offer. She said, "I'd like that, Johnny. When do you want to go?"

"Can't say yet. I'll let you know."

"Is something wrong?"

"Rotten," he said.

"What is it, Johnny?"

"I don't know," he lied. "I'm not going to wait around and find out." He turned outside, thinking of Gracie. A small anticipatory smile touched his lips, and he strode toward the stable.

Experience had taught him that neither a man's bank nor his home was safe as a hiding place for his fortune; this was why he now racked out of Antelope and put his horse on the northwesterly road along the banks of the Ash. He arrived at the limestone badlands at the head of the valley just after noon. It took him another two hours of steady, tortuous travel before he came to the face of a hundred-foot rock face. Hand-dug footholds in the cliff led upward to an immense split in the limestone wall, and it was in the ancient adobe ruins housed by that cave that he knelt to paw rocks away and dig with his hands into the junkpile left by ages of time. Presently he stood, burdened with the weight of a pair of dirt-caked, weathered saddlebags. He slung them over his shoulder and carefully descended the face of the rock wall. A waspish expression touched his lips and went away. He drew a long breath and mounted and swung back the way he had come. The horse kicked up small dust flurries which hung suspended in its wake, as though awaiting another traveler to enfold. Fargo felt a shudder touch him. He said, "Ah, my bones are tired—I'm weary of fools." He looked back along the course of his patchwork life and wondered.

By the time he reached the flats and left the badlands behind, the sun had gone down and night was complete, the moon crawled into sight before he turned into a little-

used road running southeast along the west bank of the
river. He had a sudden urge to be active, and dismounted
and started walking, leading the sorrel. He strode over the
uneven ground until his legs began to tire, then sat for a few
moments on a rock. It was then that he heard a sound in the
brush ahead; when he looked that way, he made out a
horseman moving forward on his backtrail, a shadowed
figure in the cover of the marching trees. He straightened,
wholly alert. No rider ought to be on his trail. Fear of that
man's possible identity touched him with cold fingertips,
and he stepped softly back among the cottonwoods and
halted. The rider left the far thickets and advanced, and
Fargo suddenly realized he had left his horse standing in
plain view down in the rocks. His terror grew, and he faded
farther back.

CHAPTER ELEVEN

Fear and the night were dark and oppressive. Fargo was cold and clasped his arms about himself and shivered, longing for the fire he could not build and the shelter he could not reach. Crouched behind a thick cottonwood, he wondered if the rider had recognized him. He heard him crashing around higher up on the hill and cursed silently. He told himself he had to get out of this. There was little to life—or perhaps there was a lot. Either way, he was not disposed to give it up.

The horseman was still rattling on the hilltops. Fargo stepped away from the cottonwood and started threading a southeastward path through the trees. He would cross the river somewhere below, get to town, pick up Gracie, and get out. He would find another place and another, more rewarding and less risky, game. He descended close to the Ash, to allow its rush to cover the sound of his progress. He kept as much as he could within the patchwork shadows of trees and traced a course parallel to the bank.

"Just a minute, Fargo."

He stopped; he recognized Hollister's voice and swallowed. *Not now!* He looked around slowly.

Hollister rode forward from the rocks, grinning, leading Fargo's horse. "Drop your gun and start walking."

"Where?"

"Maybe town—maybe the hotel. Shawn might be interested in this. Go on—drop the gun. I won't shoot you." Hollister grinned. "You can trust me."

"I wouldn't trust you around the far side of a toothpick."

"Drop the gun," Hollister said. He dipped the muzzle of his rifle toward Fargo.

Fargo's shoulders dropped. He let the revolver fall and stepped back away from it. Hollister said, "On the hoof."

For an instant Fargo's eyes shone with white heat; then he turned stiffly to move forward in long, abrupt strides. His heels clicked on stones; in back of him he heard the steady clipping of the two horses. "Don't tire yourself," Hollister said, and laughed.

At a point not far ahead the dim trail dipped close by the Ash before rising away through the cottonwoods. Fargo's eyes held that point while he approached. He searched the tumbling waters rushing by and made his brash decision. "What happens to me?"

"I'll leave that up to Shawn," Hollister told him. "He'll think of something."

"No doubt," Fargo agreed. "But it would be a great disappointment to me to see him do anything crude. I don't think—"

He broke in midsentence, jabbing in his heels and whirling off the dust surface of the trail, crossing the intervening rocks in a single long stride and diving flat into the curling water. He heard Hollister's first quick bullet just before his head entered the dark river, and then he was under, swimming strongly against the current. When his chest began to burn, he kicked off the bottom and shot to the surface, exhaling all the air in his lungs. His head broke the top, and he gulped in a huge gasp and flopped back into the muddy deep. That one instant above the flailing surface had shown him the equal blackness of water and land with the sky; the moon must have climbed over a cloud. This was an advantage; another was that Hollister would expect him to swim downstream with the current.

He broke surface again, more quietly this time, and kept his head above the river until he saw something move on the bank, something about a hundred yards south of him. Presently it moved away from the trees, crossed the trail, and clattered over a flat of rock—Hollister. He was drifting downstream, searching. Fargo trembled violently for a moment, caught himself, and struck out. He swam with strong strokes for the north bank, where he hoisted himself out of the water and stepped dripping into the trees.

He couldn't head for town now. The only route left open to him lay north, toward Hatchet. Perhaps he could pick up a horse from Stratemeier. *Damn!* Did Hollister know what was in the bulging saddlebags on the horse he led? One thing was sure: that fortune was lost to Fargo, at least for the moment.

* * *

Hatchet was an armed camp centered on the storage shed—the only building not burned to the ground. Overmile sat with a hip on the corner of a high crate, and Stratemeier watched him narrowly while the tall foreman pushed a ramrod into the muzzle of his rifle. Overmile said softly, "Somebody's outside."

Stratemeier nodded, having heard the same boot scratches. He cupped the lamp chimney, blew it out, and went around the packing box to the door, palming his Remington. Knuckles rapped the door; he said, "Come in," and waited. A lean shape filled the door.

"Light the lamp, Eric. I'm alone."

Fargo's voice sent a ripple of surprise through Stratemeier. He found a match and struck it on his thumbnail. Lamplight drove blackness back and Fargo shut the door quickly, running gaunt fingers through his soaked hair. Stratemeier regarded him curiously for a moment, then said to Overmile, "See if you can hunt him up some dry clothes."

"All right." Overmile spoke without enthusiasm and went around Fargo to the door.

Fargo said, "Where's your crew?"

"Two of them quit, and the rest are out trying to keep what cattle we've got left," Stratemeier answered. He considered Fargo closely—he looked like a man who had just suffered a severe fright.

"Got any dry tobacco?"

"Here. What brings you up here, Johnny?"

Fargo shook his head. He accepted the tobacco and made a cigarette; he lifted the chimney from the lamp and stooped for a light. Stratemeier saw his hands tremble. Fargo straightened and took a nervous turn around the small room. He said, "If you were to guess who burned you out, you'd be wrong, Eric."

Stratemeier's glance was narrow and direct. "Would I?"

"It wasn't Boone or any of his boys."

"How do you know that?"

Fargo dragged deeply on the smoke. "I lit the match."

Stratemeier neither moved nor changed expression. "I see."

"Listen, Eric. I didn't have much choice. I've been working on and off for Boone Shields—nothing big, but once in a while I passed on a tip to him. We both profited from it. Then Edith and Will got here, and somehow Will found out. He threatened to expose me if I didn't string along with him."

"And besides," Stratemeier murmured, "you figured you were joining the winning side."

"What if I did? A man's got to look out for himself."

"Then why come to me? You were taking a chance on dangling from a tree by coming here."

"Listen, I decided to clear out of here this morning. I was going back East. But one of Boone's men caught me on the trail this afternoon. I got away from him in the river, but he'd got every cent I own—it was on the saddle. I've only got one chance of getting that back, and that's to join your side and hope you come out on top. I can do you a lot of good. I know where Boone keeps the cattle he steals. I know where his men hide out when they're not in War Pass. I know every distribution point for the cattle his men sell. I can put the finger on his spies for you, and I can lead you to anything of his you want. All I want is a chance to get my money back and clear out of this country. Look, Eric, can't we make a deal?"

Impulse boosted Stratemeier forward; he grasped Fargo's wet collar and hauled the man up close. "Johnny, what proof is there you won't cross me as fast as you did Will?"

Fargo spoke mildly. "You'll have to take a chance on that. All I can give is my word."

"Somebody's going to pay for this ranch burning," Stratemeier growled.

"Why not the insurance company? Edith said you had it heavily covered."

"I don't have any insurance," Stratemeier said. "That's part of the same story she's been spreading in every town I've lived in. Johnny, if—"

The door opened, and Overmile swung in. His glance touched Stratemeier and then Fargo; he dropped his armload of dry work clothes on the box by the lamp. "There's a horse saddled for you by the corral."

"I don't want it," Fargo said. "I'll be staying here."

Overmile's glance reached Stratemeier and Stratemeier nodded slowly. He gestured toward the clothing. "Put that on. We'll have to—" One loud scratch sounded outside somewhere and whipped them all into silence. They heard the short noise again. Overmile said; "Somebody out there."

Stratemeier snatched up Overmile's rifle from the crate, stuffed a shell into the chamber, dropped half a box of cartridges in his pocket, and went through the door. A silhouette weaved against the sky, and Overmile called, "Who's that—who's that?"

There was no answer. The shadow faded into deeper shadows, and after a moment Stratemeier caught the sudden crush of boots on gravel. The man was down at the far end of the hollow, reaching south past the corrals, and Stratemeier called, "Look for his horse around here," and broke into a run. In a moment the fugitive broke from cover ahead, swung across into the trees, and smashed upward onto a hill slope, abandoning caution. Stratemeier gained some ground before the man entered the thicker timber. He listened a moment, heard nothing, and started moving again at a long slant, slipping quietly forward. Brush swung softly in his wake; he threaded the thicket without sound. The shadow bobbed ahead of him, splashed into the river, and swam across to the opposite shore before Stratemeier achieved the near bank. Presently the man ahead began to lose his distinct outline as the heavier hilltops beyond threw their dense blackness forward. He reached the base of the hill and left a wake of sound as he pressed through the undergrowth and climbed as rapidly as he could. When Stratemeier reached that growth, dripping with water from the Ash, he paused. The man had broken through the far side of the brush, and now Stratemeier could see his weaving shape top the hill, toward the hollow of Kathy McCune's Lucky Roll.

Stratemeier ran full tilt into the Lucky Roll yard, windmilling to keep his balance, and jumped aboard the only horse that had stayed near the gate when the fugitive had left it open. A horse was crashing off to the left. He swerved that way and suddenly the racket stopped. The fugitive was hoping to ambush him. Too impatient to wait him out, Stratemeier made a quick choice, dismounted, and slapped the horse. It ran off to the west, which would make the man think he was flanking, and Stratemeier crouched down to run low toward the direction of the fugitive's last signals.

He found him. The man sat silently among the aspens,

his gun muzzle playing warily over the scene behind him. Fear seemed to touch him; he lifted his boots to spur the horse. It was then that Stratemeier called: "Over here, bucko." He slipped out of the trees and held his rifle on the horseman.

The man spun and thumbed off two fast, unaimed shots before Stratemeier's slug caught him at the collar and lifted him off the horse.

Stratemeier draped the rifle over his forearm and came by the fugitive, who lay flat, looking up at him with blood foaming his lips and coursing down his shirt to stain the land.

"Got some water?"

Stratemeier shook his head. He watched the man lie back against the earth and saw the life flow out of his body. Presently he bent and hoisted the body onto the horse and turned to lead the pony back through the ghostly white-trunked aspens. In a few minutes he neared the edge of the trees. Crashing behind him warned of an oncoming horse, and he brought his rifle up and trained it on the depths of the grove. But it was only the bareback horse he had left a while ago, a gentle beast that trotted up to him and stood waiting. He swung aboard and led the horse with the dead man on it, using the halter and rope Hollister had snatched up.

It was well after midnight when he racked before the marshal's sign at the courthouse. McClintock came out before Stratemeier had mounted the porch; without speaking, the marshal helped him carry the body into the cell corridor. They deposited it on a bunk, staring blankly at the ceiling. McClintock seemed uncomfortable, and when he looked up at Stratemeier, there was no friendliness whatsoever in his glance. Stratemeier thought, *He's one Edith managed to convince.*

McClintock said, "Well?"

"He was snooping around Hatchet. I chased him as far as the Lucky Roll. Then he threw down on me, and I didn't have much choice. It would have been better to have him alive—he might have been able to answer a few questions."

"That's Syl Hollister," McClintock said. "Pretty high up— he was close to Boone."

Stratemeier nodded and swung toward the door. McClintock's voice stopped him: "Hold it, Stratemeier." McClintock held a cell door open. "You might as well go on in here."

"What for? Nobody would touch me for shooting a bandit like him."

"Maybe not," McClintock said, "but they sure as hell will for killing a woman. I'm arresting you for the murder of Miss Edith Rachal."

CHAPTER TWELVE

Gracie Peters advanced to stand in the doorway, a plump and friendly looking girl. With her back to the restaurant, her face to the street, she felt the gloom of her life press in around her and narrow her existence down to this drab town and this small shop. She stood with her arms crossed over her breasts and thought of Johnny Fargo. She hadn't seen him all week. What would frighten him enough to make him want to leave the country? she wondered. She remembered his invitation to come with him, though, and it brought warmth to her.

The wind along the street had been rising all morning, and Gracie had shut the windows. Now, shortly before noon, sand was whipping through town at high speed, turning the air brown and effectively keeping traffic off the streets. Miles LeVane, of the Clover mine, came in coughing, and she gave him a mug of beer. Gracie looked out the window and could not see the building fronts across the street. A shape materialized to weave blindly through the swirling storm, banged into the outside wall of the place, slid along to the door, and came in. LeVane said, "Shut that door," and came forward at a shambling run. He put his full weight against the door and got it closed. "Only a fool goes out in weather like this."

"Got caught in it a couple miles out," old Milo Teague said. Dirt caked his weathered face. "Sudden weather."

"Ain't it," agreed LeVane. "How about a beer?"

Gracie poured another mug for Teague. The front door swung open, and the gunman Shawn staggered in and whirled to push the door shut. He came forward and accepted the mug Gracie handed him. "This country can be damned rough at times."

"It can," Milo Teague said.

"This will play hell with my herds," Shawn said.

"Your herds?"

"Why," Milo Teague said, "Mr. Shawn's the new owner of Hatchet. Ain't that right, Mr. Shawn?"

"That's right," Shawn said. He lit a cigar.

Teague said, "What kind of business would bring a man to town in this blow?"

"I didn't expect to hit anything this hard," Shawn said. "I moved some grangers off Hatchet night before last. Wonder what they're up to now."

"Probably burning their wagon for warmth," Teague murmured. "Have you no feelings, Shawn?"

Shawn's lids dropped. "Whatever happens to a man, he brings upon himself."

"That's a fact," Teague murmured. He kept his gaze steady on Shawn.

"A man," Shawn said, "becomes only what he has the ambition to become. You can't sit back and wait for the world to bring it to you." He regarded Teague with a harder inspection. "You know, old man, you and I can get along if you'll let it be that way."

LeVane said, "Wait a minute—let me catch up here. I've been away for several days. Stratemeier's only been in jail a little over a week. He hasn't even been tried yet. How'd you get his ranch?"

"I took it," Shawn said.

The wind was dying outside. Morgan McClintock entered the restaurant and stopped when he saw Will Shawn. "Taking a chance coming to town, aren't you, Shawn?"

Shawn grinned. "Want to arrest me, Marshal?"

"On the day a charge is sworn against you, I'll come after you, Shawn. It would be a mistake to think otherwise."

"Sure," Shawn said. "I'll be ready for you, Marshal. Any time."

McClintock said, "I don't suppose you'd care to tell me what happened to Overmile and his crew. Or Johnny Fargo."

"The truth is, Marshal, I don't know. I haven't seen any of them."

McClintock nodded—he seemed to believe Shawn. Gracie thought it was probably because Shawn wouldn't have any reason to lie about it. If he had killed or harmed the men, he was mad enough to brag about it.

Shawn smiled again and went to the door. He pulled his hat down tight and pushed outside. Miles LeVane said,

"Marshal, something had better be done about that. Quickly."

McClintock shrugged. "I don't think he'll do any harm. He's crazy, you know. All he's doing is protecting Hatchet while Stratemeier's in jail. The only reason I arrested Stratemeier was Shawn's filing the charge against him. There's no evidence to convict him on. He's got a fair alibi, and anybody could have climbed to her window and shot her."

"But what will happen when he's released?"

McClintock swung to regard him half angrily. He leveled his gaze on LeVane and after a moment launched into a speech: "Mr. LeVane, the best thing for this country would be for it to get rid of the toughs, is that right, sir? All right—that's why I think we'll be serving our own best interests by staying strictly out of this whole mess. When Stratemeier gets out of jail, he'll declare war on Shawn. Shawn's a mad killer, and Stratemeier's a crook with a record twenty years long. Why not let them wipe each other out?"

Milo Teague placed his schooner on the counter and walked to the door. He paused with his hand on the knob. "You may be wrong about Stratemeier, Marshal. Might behoove you to check up on that so-called record of his." He swung out the door. LeVane got up and followed Teague out.

Gracie said, "Marshal, is that right about Johnny Fargo? Don't you know where he is?"

"He and Overmile and the whole Hatchet crew disappeared about the same time," McClintock said. "They haven't been seen since." Then he too left, and Gracie stood in melancholy silence.

Within his tiny cell, Stratemeier lay on a metal frame cot with his knees drawn up and his hands behind his head. Out in the corridor a single lamp flickered on low oil. He rose slowly and wrapped his fists around the bars of the high window, and watched the night. The valley of the Ash was tainted with Will Shawn's strange hatreds; and, while Stratemeier stood confined, Shawn was finally carrying out the end of Edith's revenge, a vendetta that had lasted a generation and now continued beyond her death.

Sounds drifted from the dark—boots crunching, one man's hoarse breathing, and a rattle approaching the window. Stratemeier's glance flashed to the end of the dim corridor. McClintock's office door was shut.

"How's it like in there?" Ben Overmile's voice was a hiss.

"Hot and close."

"We'll take you out of this tin can fast enough," Overmile said.

The heat of impulse urged Stratemeier to encourage Overmile's scheme, but then he said, "Forget it. Don't try to buck McClintock, Ben. He's too big for you. Who's that with you?"

"Just an unemployed gambler." Johnny Fargo wheeled out of the shadows and came forward. "You're a fool to let McClintock keep you in there, Eric. Shawn's got this thing rigged against you from top to bottom. If Will ever had any sanity, it's left him now. He's parked on Hatchet with half of Boone Shields' crew, just inviting anybody to try moving him off."

"Let him park there for a while. Listen, Johnny, if I start running, there'll be a bounty on my head. That's exactly what Will wants."

"Don't worry so damn much about Shawn," Overmile said. "Worry about saving your own skin."

"My skin's all right, Ben." Overmile's lip was curling, as though in contempt, and Stratemeier said, "Stay camped where you are, Ben. We'll just wait this out—and there's all the time in the world for moving Will off Hatchet. Don't get anxious."

"Sure," Overmile said. "Have it your way. But I figure you're invitin' a good share of grief. I'll see you in court." He swung into the shadows.

It was not until all sound of Overmile's travel had died that Fargo spoke again. "Eric, you look like you're still hunting for the right-sized shovel to dig your hole in the world. You look like you tried the wrong size—and they caught you for it."

"Meaning I should just let Shawn have Hatchet and get my tail out of the country before he burns it?"

"Maybe," Fargo said. "I'm trying to save you some of that grief Ben was talking about. With Boone behind him Will swings a lot of weight."

"And a wide loop," Stratemeier said. "But Will's insane. Sooner or later he'll get in over his head. When he slips, I want to be there to catch him."

Fargo shook his head. "Listen. This started because of Edith. But she's dead now. This business has gotten too big for a handful of us. You'd be smart to clear out—"

"Quit talking in circles. If you're planning on see-sawing back to the other side, Johnny, say so. If you want to get back on Will's side, you'll have to take the same risks he takes."

"No," Fargo said. "I'm still with you. I've got no choice. That was just honest advice. Look, are you sure you don't want to bust out of here?"

"I'm sure."

"All right," Fargo said, his tone uncertain. He dropped away from the window and disappeared.

Behind Stratemeier the door to the front office opened, allowing a long splash of light to come down the hallway. Morgan McClintock said, "I figured they'd try some fool stunt like that."

"Too bad they didn't go ahead, eh, Marshal?"

"Why, I guess it would have made things simple," McClintock admitted. "By the way, where's the insurance investigator to look over that burn at Hatchet?"

"No investigator coming," Stratemeier said. "No insurance."

McClintock frowned briefly. After a moment he advanced to the cell door. He took a sack of Bull Durham from his pocket and tossed it on the cot. "You may run out."

"Thanks."

"That was Fargo and Overmile, wasn't it?"

"Yes. Why?"

McClintock shrugged. "I wondered where they'd gone to. Funny—I didn't figure Fargo to join your team. Not ever. That's two mistakes I've made in this thing. The other is believing that Rachal woman's story about your record."

"A good many people have believed that one, Marshal. It's easy to bluff a lie through from a podium."

"Sure enough. But it's my business to know better." McClintock turned back along the corridor and shut the door. Darkness returned, the corridor's single flickering lamp almost out of oil. Stratemeier heard McClintock's voice dim from behind the forward door: "Come on in— Sure enough, in this way. He's up."

The door opened once more, and Kathy McCune came along the corridor. "Eric?"

He realized she couldn't see him in the darkness of the cell. He moved up to the barred door and wrapped both fists around the bars, high above his head, leaning against his upflung arms. She advanced, her face in complete shadow. She said, "Bring your hands down."

His fists slid down along the bars until she could reach them; she covered them with her hands and brought her face close enough for him to see her eyes. She said, "I'm sending Frank Royal to Prescott for a lawyer."

He shook his head. "No use."

"Are you going to rot in here to please Will Shawn?"

"You know," he said, "and I know. But prove it—prove it was Shawn. No lawyer can do that. No, Kathy. My thanks, but I'll sit it out. I want to be freed by a court of law—and then watch Shawn crumble."

"You mean make him crumble."

"Maybe," he said. He swung his back to her and thrust his hands deep in his pockets. "Don't get yourself involved, Kathy. Forget I ever talked to you. Keep out of my grief."

Her answer was soft and very sure. "I can't."

"It will only turn you sour. Listen, Kathy. This thing started with death twenty years ago, and the only way it can end now is with more dying. Don't trespass in this fight—"

"In other words," she said, "you don't want me. Is that it?"

He turned to face her, and when he answered, his tone was as cool and deliberate as he could make it; "That's it—I don't want you." And when she did not answer, he felt the life go out of him and the cold come in.

But finally she said, "I don't believe you. But I'll stay out, if it's what you really want."

"I don't want you to get hurt. You can't buy into this, Kathy. It's not your trouble."

"Isn't it?" She didn't wait for his answer; she turned quickly and strode out of the hall. Her head was down; her shoulders were raised. He wasn't sure, but he thought she was crying.

A thick traffic of men blossomed from the door of the Stockmen's Theatre and dispersed to speckle the street. Clay Videen paused beside the doorway and waited a few moments until the marshal stepped out. "Marshal, this gives you all the authority we can muster. You've got to go

up there and find enough evidence to hang Shields and
every tough in War Pass. We can't afford to waste any more
time."

"I am not a magician, Mr. Videen. I'll do what I can."
McClintock swung off the boardwalk and quartered across
to the courthouse, where he looked in on Stratemeier and
then sat at his desk to clean his rifle. He spoke mildly to
himself.

"Everybody knows Boone's been long-looping Ash River
cows. Now, why is it nobody ever caught him with a single
head of cattle with a blotted brand?"

He unscrewed the sideplates from the Winchester's
action and dropped small pearls of oil on the action. "Surely
is strange. How in hell could a man blot out that big
Hatchet brand out of a cow's hide without making it
obvious? He could do it if his own brand was bigger, but
Boone's is just average sized. How in hell does he do it?
Only one answer," he murmured. "He must steal the calves
before they're branded. But suppose he does, now. What
do you think their mothers would be doing? Raising all
kinds of hell. McClintock, since when does a mother cow
let a rustler walk away with her calf? But I've never found a
Hatchet cow up in the hills where it might have trailed its
calf.

"Now, suppose Boone steals both the mother cows and
the unbranded calves. Suppose he keeps them all hidden
together until the calves are weaned. Then say he brands
the calves with his own iron and drives the mother cows
back down to Hatchet. That way he doesn't risk branding
fires on Hatchet, he doesn't blotch brands, and he's not
caught with odd cow-calf bunches. Anybody that saw a
Shield calf following a Hatchet cow around would know the
truth. But not if he cut the cows out and drove them home
after the calves were weaned. Sure enough. That's the
answer. Find the place where he hides the calves with their
mothers, or find the place where he hides the stolen
bullion, and we'll pin the tail on the jackass for sure."

CHAPTER THIRTEEN

The surcharged clouds were dense and sullen brown in color when Morgan McClintock pushed his blaze-faced black out of Antelope, heading west toward the Topaz summits, and a rain was drifting down when, in the late afternoon, he put his black boldly into the center of the winding street of War Pass. He stepped down before the saloon, opened the heavy log door, and went in.

The room was empty. He took off his hat and went immediately to the glowing Franklin in the center of the floor. Warm currents swept around him when he spread his hands above it, palms down. It was strange, the great spread of temperature from the valley of the Ash to the Topaz peaks. The glow showing through the stove's isinglass was much more comfortable than the hot flame showing in the stove at the cold-blooded Satterlee's Mercantile in Antelope. The room held a faint odor of whisky, and he tipped his hat back and helped himself to a drink at the bar. Then called, "Come out here, Boone."

He swallowed the drink and put his eyes on the door opening through the side of the room into the kitchen. Shields bulled through, wearing a petulant expression on his big face, and walked around McClintock. "Hullo, Morg." He spoke sourly and laid down his customary warning: "This place don't cater to badges."

It was more a matter of protocol than a real threat, and McClintock did not bother to answer. He went back to the stove and stood, legs apart and arms extended over the Franklin. Shields said, "Go find your horse and hightail."

"Just as soon as I get what I came for." McClintock dropped his arms to his sides and turned to face Shields squarely. "Have you seen him?"

"Who?"

"Come on, Boone. Don't play games."

Shields grunted. "You're draggin' your picket, Morg. Go home."

"In time," McClintock said. "In time. He's got two fingers missing on his left hand. Riding a blue mare with a Hashknife mark. Tall fella."

Boone leaned carelessly on the bar. He smiled and pronounced his words slowly: "What his name?"

"Jack Drury. From El Paso."

"What you want him for?"

McClintock shrugged and stood waiting. Boone said, "Morg, this is silly. We're both playin' the same game, and we both know exactly what's going to be said before anybody says a word. Your rules make you come up here and ask the questions. My rules make me keep my mouth shut. If Drury's here, I won't say anything anyway. What's the point?"

"If he's not here, you might tell me that," McClintock observed. "And that could help."

Boone grinned. "Well, now, maybe I've seen him and maybe I ain't. Either way, if he got this deep into the mountains, he's safe. You might as well leave him be, Morg. You know better than to try and get a man out of my country."

"Maybe not. I've never made a test of it."

"Don't. Listen, bucko, Antelope don't want a dead marshal."

McClintock's smile was mild, then grew tight. "Which one of the boys was it that burned down Hatchet?"

"You're crazy."

"Well," McClintock said, "maybe I am. That doesn't answer the question."

Boone shrugged blandly. "Why ask me questions like that, Morg? The only reason I'm still runnin' this place is I'm the only man in these hills that everybody up here trusts."

"Which is a hell of a comment on human nature," McClintock murmured.

Boone's smile showed his brown teeth. "Sure enough. I'm a rascal, Morg. But I like it."

"Do you?" McClintock's glance probed steadily against him, but Boone had his guard lifted against it. McClintock said, "Well, thanks a heap for the help, Boone. I'll see you sometime."

"Any old time, Morg. *Mi casa esta de usted.*"

"Sure." McClintock walked stiff-legged to the door. He

mounted his black and regarded the face of the weathered saloon. Boone Shields would be the same till the day he died. McClintock smiled at that, and at his own invention of a Jack Drury, as he rode into the steady drizzle.

Boone pushed forward from the bar and went around into the kitchen. From the back door he called, "Naco."

Naco came up from the stable down canyon and walked forward. "What'd he want this time?"

"He's lookin' for Jack Drury."

"Who's that?"

"Beats the hell out of me."

"Ain't no such gent," Naco decided promptly.

"What?"

"This Drury," Naco said. "McClintock needed an excuse to come up here and poke around. So he made up a fellow on the dodge. I told you the committee gave him the go-ahead to pin you to the wall."

Boone nodded slowly. "I've been lyin' to him for years, and I know he knows it. But usually he puts up more of a fight. Guess you're right. I've tolerated him long enough. I think it's about time for Morg."

"I guess so," Naco said. "I'll see you later." He swung back down the muddy alley to the stable. He saddled his pinto and rode down the gorge, a squat and bitter-faced man, looking ahead at Morgan McClintock. He cut off the trail and galloped toward the higher reaches. Half an hour later he pulled up at the Hollister shack and called out. While he waited he had a look at the bunch of horses penned in the corral—Milo Teague's horses. Buck Hollister, brother of the dead Syl, appeared in the shack doorway, chewing on a matchstick. Naco laid his flat stare on him. "Kind of risky, keepin' those animals here, ain't it?"

"I got to drift them over by stages to avoid losin' some," Hollister said. "I'll get them over the hump tonight."

"Forget that. Seen McClintock?"

"Sure. I been one jump ahead of him all day."

"You might get a jump behind him and see he don't find out anything."

"I might," Hollister agreed. "You ride over and tell Sim Haven to get his tail over here and watch these horses."

"All right." Naco swung the pinto around and swept into the trees.

* * *

Morgan McClintock descended a steep grade and trotted around to the start of a dead-end gorge. There was a good chance this was the hiding place where calves were weaned and branded with the Shield. A thick brush fence efficiently enclosed the mouth of the high-walled canyon, and he unmounted and set to work clearing away a small passage in the fence. He had just remounted the black when a sound came forward along the ground—hoofbeats advancing. The shout of a bullet was his next warning of company. He threw his head up and for an instant stared at the slopes to either side of the canyon mouth; there was a quick break of expression on his weathered face. He whirled the black away from the brush fence, into the timber. Ahead of him a horseman broke from the farther pine grove and flung his horse around, also reaching for the trees.

In the shelter, McClintock peered ahead and moved in the direction of the ambusher, hearing a horse whip through the timber. He had to settle this before the outpost in the cabin upcanyon got down here. He lost the sound of motion, and caution made him pull up. The rider, he decided, must not be too far off, and then, suddenly, he found the man. Buck Hollister sat wide and heavy not fifty feet from him. McClintock muttered, "Not the time for niceties," and pulled off a shot that took Hollister in the right shoulder and twisted him half around. McClintock whipped his horse forward to thread the intervening trees at a run. When he saw Hollister's gun lifting, he brought his own sights to bear. Flame mushroomed out of the barrel, and Hollister spun off his saddle.

McClintock punched two fresh cartridges into his gun and wheeled toward the opening he had made in the brush fence. The guard would be up by now, wondering what the shooting was all about.

But when he arrived at the shack, there was no one inside, and no horse nearby. The outpost had cleared out. McClintock shrugged and, keeping his gun ready, moved out into the meadow to have a look at some brands.

CHAPTER FOURTEEN

In the morning, after he had eaten a fried meal brought over from Gracie's, Stratemeier saw McClintock coming down the hall with Will Shawn. The gunman's glance was slightly contemptuous. McClintock swung the cell door open, admitted Shawn, and locked the door again before he left the corridor.

Shawn did not speak until the far door closed. Stratemeier had a glimpse of the man's bright, bold eyes before Shawn dropped his lids carefully and spoke with blunt coolness. "A prisoner has damned few friends, Eric. I want you to know who yours are."

"I see none here," Stratemeier said.

"Don't get rash with me, Eric. You're in no position for it. This country has a way of treating men who kill women."

"You're pious this morning, Will," Stratemeier murmured. "Especially since we both know who killed Edith."

"Maybe I know," Shawn said. "But you're just guessing." He smiled.

"Go on."

"I want to make you a deal, Eric."

"You've got the floor," Stratemeier said.

"I signed the complaint against you. I'm the only one that can withdraw it."

"And you will, provided I do what you want."

"Exactly." He ticked his conditions off on his fingers. "One, you clear out of the country when I let you go. Two, you sign over Hatchet to me. And three, you keep your mouth shut—your word on that."

The suggestion of a smile touched Stratemeier's lips. "Will, you're riding pretty high right now. But your cinch is about to break."

He could see color enrich Shawn's cheeks; the man's gaze was suddenly wicked. "Do you want trouble with me, Eric?"

"I've been having trouble with you for twenty years."

"If that's a threat, Eric, I'll remember it. Don't forget I gave you your chance."

Shawn turned away to face the barred door, but Stratemeier's voice caught him and turned him reluctantly around.

"Will!"

Stratemeier leaped forward, his first chopping down at the angle of Shawn's neck, his other hand plunging toward the man's holstered gun. Before Shawn could act, Stratemeier had the gun in his fist and stood back, regarding Shawn mildly. "Sit down, Will, and we'll wait for the marshal."

"Do you think you can get away with this in broad daylight?"

"Why not?"

Shawn shrugged abruptly and sat on the bunk. "I'm on top now," he said, "and all of a sudden you're acting like every other crummy cowboy. Look, Eric, you're insane to try a jailbreak. They'll hunt you down like a rabid coyote. There'll be a price on you. Are you out of your head?"

"I guess that's my worry," Stratemeier said. "I'll leave the country, all right—after I've seen you gone to hell the hard way." He used his words as a whip against Shawn's forced blandness.

Shawn broke out of it. "What's mine is mine, Eric! Stay away from it!"

Stratemeier smiled. "Let's see how long you can hang onto it, Will." He balanced the revolver easily in his hand, and backed into the cell corner that McClintock would not be able to see when he entered the corridor.

The marshal did not take too long. When Stratemeier heard his footsteps in the corridor, he trained the gun on Shawn; and when McClintock confronted the door, Stratemeier spoke easily: "Hold it. Drop your guns on the floor. Easy. Kick them away from you."

McClintock complied, moving with careful deliberation; he seemed amused. Stratemeier said, "Now unlock the door and come on in."

McClintock obeyed again. He left the keyring dangling in the iron lock. Shawn spoke softly through gritted teeth: "I'll bring this whole damned country down around your ears."

Stratemeier stepped out, locked the door, and took the key ring. "Sorry, Marshal."

"I'll have to hunt you down," McClintock said.

"I expect you will," Stratemeier said, and turned. It was then that Shawn leaped forward to grip the bars. His lips pulled back to show his teeth; he spoke in a strained voice: "Eric, maybe you ought to know it wasn't Warren Rachal that raped your sister."

Stratemeier's eyes touched Shawn's; his jaw rippled, but otherwise he gave no sign of response. He shut the door behind him, dropped the keys on the desk, and started searching the office. He found his own gun and belt in a drawer and buckled them on. For a moment he hesitated, frowning. McClintock had given him this chance by allowing Shawn into the cell with a gun, but he had precious little time to make use of it. It was clearly a choice between leaving the country, wanted, or hiding within it to prove his innocence and regain Hatchet.

It was Shawn's parting remark that decided him; he would need time to consider its implications. But conceding the possibility that the madman might have been speaking the truth, only one man could know the truth—the man who killed Janice.

Twilight smudged the outlines of the Topaz summits. Stratemeier circulated among the aspens, pushing his sorrel up the giant staircase of the mountains. All during the day he had caught occasional sight of horsemen riding the hills; not all of them were hunting him, but some must be—Shawn's Hatchet riders and townsmen recruited by McClintock, and possibly some of Boone's bandits. Once he had spotted McClintock's black, and another time he had seen Naco's unmistakable brown shape threading through the forest clearings far below him.

By midnight he was climbing a canyon into a high-rising pass, pressing steadily deeper into the Topaz fastness until at last he reached a ridge crest from which he could look down on War Pass. Shadowed by the mountain, the ramshackle town looked ghostly and cold. "That's Naco again," he murmured, seeing an ant-sized shape leave one building below and cross to another.

Time stretched while Stratemeier surveyed War Pass. A number of windows winked with lamps coming on inside, and once a large mass of horsemen left the stable and breasted the saloon. One of them went inside and reappeared in a short while, and then the whole bunch left town with a heavy drumming.

Stratemeier backed the sorrel off the crest and rode back into the pines, circling to come into the street from its base. Darkness was full, clouds coming up to obscure the stars. The lights of War Pass blinked in his face, and the horses in the corral, hearing his approach, began to move restlessly. He curled around the bend of the street and dropped off boldly before the saloon. One man's high, flat shape retreated around the far corner of the stable. Two others rose in unison from chairs on the sagging saloon veranda. Boone was there, but it was Naco's voice that laid a toneless challenge on Stratemeier: "What do you want?"

The saloon door stood open, inner light casting a butter-colored gleam through to the street. When Stratemeier stepped onto the porch he had to cross that light, and Naco's tones whipped again out of the shadow: "By God! You sure as hell got your gall."

Boone and Naco both rose, both stood flat in the deep shadows. Stratemeier stood motionless, searching the street. There was that one man who had retreated around the stable; now he was probably waiting in that obscurity. And now a number of men emerged from various shadows and collected below the porch, silently curious and ominously silent. Boone Shields had not spoken yet. His breathing came hard, and Naco was still and deadly. Stratemeier caught all of this—what it was and what it meant. A thin whisper of emotion went through him, increasing his trained wariness. He walked boldly through the doorway, talking mildly: "Boone. Come in here." And turned to face the door.

Naco came in first and swung to the side of the doorframe as Boone walked forward. Naco said, "Stratemeier, you got gall enough for a buffalo." Boone shut the door and rested his meaty body there. He took on an air of saturnine indifference, chose to say nothing. Stratemeier said, "Where's Shawn?"

"How should I know?" Naco said. "This ain't his usual hangout."

"He was headed up this way this afternoon," Stratemeier said. "How close would I be if I guessed there was a new boss of War Pass, Boone?" His voice matched Naco's for dryness. Then he stopped talking. A rider was pounding forward along the street, his horse's fast-striking hoofs pounding the hard earth. That rider trotted to the saloon and called out, his voice carrying clearly in through the walls: "Boone!"

Stratemeier kept watch on Boone. The man put his hands in his pockets and stood with his legs apart. A man outside ran along the porch and stopped; someone spoke softly out there. Boone's eyes, cold and calculating, watched Stratemeier's expression. The man just arrived in the street was being warned of Stratemeier's presence. Stratemeier lifted his voice: "Come on in, Will."

There was a hard pounding on the porch; the knob turned, the door swung open, pushing Boone aside; and Will Shawn, up from his kingdom on Hatchet, came in and shut the door. He stood beside Boone. He said quickly, "What the hell?"

Stratemeier neither moved nor spoke; and after a moment Shawn smiled. "You're a good guesser, Eric. You knew you'd never catch me unguarded on Hatchet."

"Maybe," Stratemeier murmured.

Naco said, "But where does it put you?"

Boone's dark, moon-shaped face had gone blank, and now only his eyes showed feeling as they rolled from Naco to Shawn, and then back to Stratemeier. Naco said again, "So now what have you got?"

"Another piece of the puzzle," Stratemeier murmured. "The Hollister boys are both dead, and so is Arnie Ward. That's just the beginning."

"Munguia and Charley Sharpe are dead, too," Boone murmured. "And so are you."

"Maybe," Stratemeier said, gravely. And suddenly a thought dropped into the room, filling the saloon with its muskiness. It loosened Naco's lips, fashioning them into an evil-shining grin. Prompted by the same impulse, Boone Shields stirred away from Shawn; and Shawn, struck by the edge of that traveling thought, moved gracefully back into the room. Stratemeier looked at him. The three men now formed a triangle with Stratemeier abruptly in the middle of it. His long jaw crept forward, and his tone turned cool and dangerous. "Move over to the bar. I want my eyes on you."

With a high glint in his eyes, Naco cast a quick glance

at Boone. Boone watched Shawn, and Shawn stood very quiet, weighing the picture in his mind. He was wholly still until Stratemeier said, "I believe I'm faster than you are, Will. I'm willing."

There was something in the way he said it. Shawn felt it; his head jerked slightly, and he said, "Wait." He cast a quick look at Boone and shook his head almost imperceptibly. "Boone, hold it. Come over here."

Boone walked forward. "Well?"

"Come here, Naco."

Moved by impatience, Shawn walked around Boone to the bar, thus losing for the three of them the crossfire advantage they had held. Now they stood before Stratemeier, with Shawn nearest the door. He reached his hand out slowly and opened it.

Out on the porch the cautious shadows of the War Pass gunmen pressed forward; they ranged out beyond the veranda, waiting for the expected sign. But no one moved, and Shawn, who was in command, was uncertain, the strange movements of his bent mind confused. Stratemeier knew that every pair of eyes was making a target of him. Then Boone spoke, in a voice that seemed touched with admiration and hatred together. "It was a damn foolish move to ride in here alone, Stratemeier. I regret you had to give it to us this easy."

"I've made you no gift yet, Boone."

"Sounds tough," Naco said.

Boone spoke in a careful drone. "I guess you're done now, Stratemeier. Want it easy or hard?"

Up to now, Shawn had hardly spoken. Now his hand flipped the heavy door shut and said, "Not yet, Boone. He had a reason for coming here, and it wasn't suicide. I want to know what he's up to."

Boone touched the knife by his waist and grinned. "One way to find out."

"How's that?"

"Ask him," Boone murmured, still grinning.

Shawn turned to face Stratemeier squarely. "Take your gunbelt off, Eric."

Stratemeier did not move. But while his eyes were on Shawn, Naco had the chance to draw his revolver; and thus commanded, Stratemeier obeyed. The smile on his cheeks did not change. He stepped back until his shoulder touched the wall. When he looked at Shawn, the cold came in from outside; the man was completely mad; but in that madness rested Stratemeier's only chance. He faced Naco's gun, but most of his attention was on Shawn. He spoke gently: "You've got me. Now what do you do with me?"

"Kind of set on a quick trigger, ain't you?" Boone laughed. "You're awful anxious to die, bucko." His beady glance settled on Shawn for a moment, and slid off. Stratemeier calmly built a cigarette and lit it. "You've never killed a man unarmed, Will. Only women. Two of them."

"That's right," Shawn said mildly, and only then realized his mistake. The deadly gaze of Boone pinned itself on him; Naco's mouth opened and the muzzle of his revolver swung half around. Stratemeier stood still and watched. "Twenty years ago you raped a girl and left her dead on the floor. That was my sister. And three weeks ago you shot a woman in her bed. That was Edith. How many others, Will?"

Shawn's voice was high and thin. "Shut up—shut up."

By then Boone had advanced along the backbar to stand behind Shawn; Shawn whirled away from the bar and put his back to the door. The attentions of Boone and Naco were hard on him; these were men who lived lives beyond the farthest frontiers of law, but nevertheless had their own strange codes. Boone said, "I guess we made a mistake, Naco."

"I guess so," Naco said.

There was a new challenge in the room now, a fight that was leaving Stratemeier completely out. Shawn strode half the length of the room to kneel by the gunbelt Stratemeier had dropped. He lifted the Remington from its holster and advanced to place it carefully on the table by Stratemeier, not a foot from Stratemeier's hand.

"Take it and shoot," Shawn said. "An even break."

Stratemeier smiled and did not move. "Never play against a stacked deck." He glanced at Boone and Naco.

Boone was nodding. "Smart," he said.

Shawn cursed and flung to the floor. Stratemeier watched him push feverishly through the crowd of gunmen to his horse.

Boone walked to the door and pushed it shut and swung to look at Stratemeier. "You knew what we'd do," he said, "and you knew what he'd do. I never seen the like."

Naco was nodding. He seemed almost to be relieved.

Boone said, "I never saw a man could work another man that close."

Outside, the drum of Shawn's horse died in the distance. Boone said, "Naco, put your gun on the bar and back away from it."

The rise of yellow anger signaled from Naco's eyes, but he uncocked the revolver and placed it on the plank and stepped away. Boone lifted his own gun from its holster and did the same. He said, "Pick up your gun and get the hell out of here."

Stratemeier knelt for his Remington. When he stood, Naco said, "It was still a damn stupid move to ride in here alone."

"Maybe not," Boone said. "Stratemeier, I don't underestimate men. I give a man what he deserves. I never liked the cut of Shawn, and I figure maybe you and him can nuisance each other right out of the country, which will save all of us here a lot of grief. But if you ever come to War Pass again, you bring your prayer book with you."

Naco nodded. "Watch your back—always."

Boone walked to the door and stepped forward where the watching cordon of men could see him. Stratemeier came through the door; Boone gave way, not making motions. Stratemeier walked down with sure strides to his horse and climbed up. No one moved. Alert and taut, Stratemeier sat tall on the sorrel, his hand resting against his gun. Then Boone spoke: "Go on—go on."

Stratemeier nodded. He pulled away from the porch and held the shapes of the standing gunmen with his attention while he drifted the sorrel into the street and walked it carefully away.

On the porch, Naco was still petulant. "You shouldn't have let him go."

"We'll never see another bucko the likes of him," Boone said. "There's other places, other times. We had him, we let him go. If we have to, we'll get him again. But I never had a night like this before. That man don't deserve to die dirty." He spoke softly and then turned back inside. "Go on back up to Buck Hollister's. Run those Teague horses down to Kingman and get us a good price. Now get out of here."

CHAPTER FIFTEEN

After a night in a hastily constructed lean-to on a talus slope, Stratemeier spent most of the gray forenoon cruising around the mountains within a seven-mile radius of War Pass, accomplishing no more than evading the searchers who seemed to be everywhere. At four o'clock finding an opening in the search net, he aimed the sorrel down the switchbacks of a game trail, heading obliquely toward the valley of the Ash.

A third of the way down he heard the drum of hoofs advancing from below, and pulled off into a thick clump of aspen. Presently, a rider, sitting a Hatchet-branded horse, drifted past, a rifle tilted indolently over his shoulder. One of Shawn's imported gunmen. Stratemeier watched him trot by; impulse and caution chased each other across his face; but he let the tough go on, deciding to save his questions for someone who had the answers.

Stratemeier wondered how far McClintock's half-hearted chase had taken the marshal, and he knew it was Hatchet and Shawn's men, not the law, that he had to fear. He gigged the sorrel and cantered across the gently undulating hills and bowed his course to come onto a ridge overlooking Bear Creek Canyon, where Overmile's camp ought to be. He could see a small group of horsemen sitting in the shadow of a cottonwood clump above the camp. "Thought so," Stratemeier said. "They're keeping watch on Overmile, expecting him or Fargo to get in touch with me. Well, good luck, boys."

He wheeled off the hillside and ran up the trough of a shallow arroyo, heading northwest, paralleling the Ash until, at sunset, he came to the first fringe of the badlands. Sharply eroded miniature mesas dotted the district, intercut by hundreds of tortuous gulches and rugged crosshills. He headed into the maze and, an hour after dark, dropped through a square cut to the bank of the Ash and rode a short distance downstream to a point at the base of a high cliff perforated with erosion caves. This would do for tonight. He ground-hitched the sorrel within a grease-wood clump and walked down to the river's edge to wash. He rose from the bank and just then heard the *clipclop* of a single set of hoofs rising over the murmur of the river. He palmed his gun and backed into the brush, keening the dark with his eyes.

The rider came upstream along the bank, riding apparently without purpose; and in the dimness Stratemeier recognized the roan gelding before he recognized the rider. He stepped forward into the open.

"Eric?"

He holstered the gun and walked forward. "Kathy—what the devil are you doing up here?"

"Looking for you," she said. "I figured if all the posses were busy hunting the mountains, that was where you wouldn't be. So I've been riding the badlands. I knew sooner or later you'd find me." She dismounted and turned to face him. "I'm glad they haven't found you."

He touched her arm. "Come on up." He took her elbow and guided her up the slope to the first of the eroded caves. He said, "You shouldn't have come."

"I know." Her slight smile brought forth the faintly quizzical look he had noted before. She said, "I brought some things I thought you might need—food, ammunition, tobacco. It's on the horse."

He nodded and crouched back against the coarse wall. She said, "Eric, what's wrong?"

His face turned dismal and gray; he said, "You can take all the justice in the world and fit it into a thimble."

She looked at the cave floor. "You're feeling a little sorry for yourself."

Her eyes rose suddenly, perhaps to catch his expression; and he said, "It's not exactly that. But I've run out of cheeks to turn. Shawn's railroaded me into a hole, and the only way I can get out is to get him in. The trouble is, he's not really responsible for what he's done. His mind has snapped."

Her mouth stirred; her eyes were moist. She said, "Miles LeVane and Ross Thompson and I got together with Videen. We're sending a consolidated wagon train of ore out this week with a twenty-man guard."

"Good luck," he said softly.

"Eric, be careful."

"Unnecessary advice," he muttered.

"But it matters to me." She moved forward to touch him. "Eric."

"What?"

"There's something else that matters to me."

"What's that?"

"You." She touched his chest and came forward. She whispered. "Is there a way out of this, for you?"

"I don't know."

"What will you do tomorrow?"

"Plant a trail for them to follow," he said. "I want to get that crew far enough away so that I can reach Shawn without having to fight through his guards."

Her hand slid up his chest to rest by his throat; the sweet smell of her hair was in his nostrils, the soft touch of her body against his own. She said, "Maybe he's too much for you to fight, Eric."

"No. Someone's got to do it. And I'm the one he's taken everything from."

"It wouldn't be so terribly wrong to run," she said.

"Don't try to change me, Kathy."

"Oh," she whispered, "I wouldn't—but I'm selfish, Eric; I couldn't bear to see you hurt any more by this. I want you to myself, as you are."

"I've been running all my life," he said. "If I don't stop now, I'll never be any good, Kathy. For you or for myself."

"Everyone knows what Shawn has done," she said. "If you hunt him down, they'll think it's only revenge and you'll be treated like an outlaw, a gunman, the rest of your life. They'll turn you bitter, Eric; you'll die alone and they won't care."

He shook his head. "Kathy, I wish—" Her hand rose to touch his lips, and she moved around to press more heavily against him. Her lips brushed his. He held her face in both hands and made his kiss gentle. Her hand caressed his stubbled cheek. The dry scratch of that sound close to his ear made him smile; and this slight bit of cheer seemed to ease some of the bitterness in him.

She turned beside him and reached out to him. His lips met hers, and he felt himself descending into a bottomless abyss, dark and infinite but still somehow protecting and warm.

* * *

He awoke an hour before dawn and rose carefully to avoid waking Kathy. He sat in the cave mouth, sitting back on his heels, packed his pipe. He was about to strike a match when he was arrested by the sound of distant scratching. His eyes whipped around to the south.

"What was that?"

"I don't know," he said. "Lie still." He sat poised by the opening, and after a moment left the cave and scrambled up the slope to the top of the rise. It did not take long to spot the four riders a bit less than a mile down the river. He descended to the cave. "Only one crowd would be coming this way. And we're too close to try outriding them. Come on."

"Where?"

"The river." The rataplan of horses grew steadily closer. He took her hand and led her quickly along the bank and stepped into the water. He held his arms up to her. "Let's go."

Her face was puzzled, but she came in, trusting him. He took her hand and waded along the bank, north thirty yards to a point where the eroded bank sloped sharply to meet the water and lay overgrown by brush. They ducked under and swam awkwardly to the bank, then sat in water up to their necks, head concealed by the root system of a bushy creosote growing out of the crumbling bank. "It's terribly cold," she said.

"I know. But we couldn't chance staying in the cave. That's where they'll be looking. We can only hope the horses don't give us away."

Hoofbeats reached a crescendo above their heads; then stopped. He heard a voice: "Cave up there, Will."

"Have a look." That was Will Shawn. Stratemeier heard a horse clatter away from the bank, going up the slope. There was no sound for a full minute; then the horse came back down. Stratemeier felt Kathy shivering; he slid his arm around her shoulders and drew her to him.

"Been someone there," the man said. "Maybe he's gone back into the malpais farther."

"Let's find out," Shawn said. "Damn! I wish a man could track in this stuff. We're going to have to comb this whole district."

"Don't get impatient, boss. We'll flush him sooner or later."

"Sure. But how old will we be?" Hoofs began chipping the shale.

Stratemeier looked at Kathy. Her jaw was tight, to keep her teeth from chattering. He felt the cold himself. He waited a while longer and said, "All right. Duck under." He found her hand and they went under to get by the thick roots hanging out over their heads.

When he surfaced, he shook his head vigorously, spraying water from his hair and clearing his ears. He smiled at her. She pulled him hard against her, groaning and clenching his back. He felt the pounding of the blood in her cheeks, the heavy rise and fall of her breathing. She didn't speak; she rolled her head and drew his lips to hers in a frenzied kiss. Her eyes were round, looking up at him. At last she said, "Deep tLoughts. What are they about, Eric?"

But he shook his head. "Time to get out of here," he said, and rose.

She came along with him to the horses, tethered back in a brushy side canyon; she touched his arm, and when he turned she said, "You know I'm in love with you, don't you?"

"Yes." He bent his head and kissed her gently. "Ride home and wait for me." He gathered the reins in quick sychronization with his rise to the saddle and swept away along the southward-reaching bank of the Ash.

The sun was down, and by eight-thirty Gracie's restaurant was empty. Johnny Fargo entered, moved to the counter, and sat quite silent, enjoying a brief smile while he watched Gracie, her back to him, arranging pies on the shelves. Then she turned; pleasure rose to her cheeks; and she leaned happily over the counter to kiss him. "Johnny."

"I'm sorry I didn't send you some kind of word," he said.

"I've missed you. But it's all right now." For a moment there were tears in her eyes; she brushed them away with a corner of her apron. "I'll bet you'd like dinner, after I've cleaned up the whole place. Wouldn't you?"

"I could always go to the Chinaman's," he suggested.

"Over my dead body." She swung her plump hips across the room and disappeared into the kitchen. When she came back, Fargo was smiling slightly. He felt her eyes on him while he ate; she regarded him with open warmth and not a little possessiveness. That had once bothered him; now it only comforted him. Gracie was round and simple, clean and honest, and wholly comfortable for a man. Fargo said, "I'm damned if I know why, but I want you to be my wife."

She took his coffee cup and went to refill it and came back. She said, "My it took you a long time to get around to saying that, Johnny."

He sat back and stared at her in completely baffled wonder. "For a while," he said, "I thought I had you figured out."

She shook her head, smiling. "A woman never lets her man figure her out, Johnny. If she stops being a mystery to him, she stops attracting him."

"Well," he observed, "in that case, carry on, woman."

He finished his meal in silence; Gracie looked on happily and finally said, "Where will we go?"

"Damned if I know. Far from here."

"Soon?"

"I hope so. First I've got to collect a debt, and I'd like to see Eric back on Hatchet before I go."

The door opened; the old habit of inspection turned Fargo's head that way. And then he rose to face Will Shawn. Shawn said, "You shouldn't have come to town, Johnny. I told you what would happen if you crossed me."

Fargo's shoulders dropped. "Gracie, you'd better stand aside." Not understanding this at all, she moved to the counter, and watched both of them, frowning. Fargo said, "Go on, Will. Get it over with."

"Draw your gun, Johnny. I don't shoot a man cold turkey."

"Why, then, I guess you'll have to, Will. I'm not pulling my gun on you."

"You'll pull it," Shawn said. He crossed the room in deliberate strides, lifted his hand carefully, and slapped Fargo's cheek with a crisp blow. Fargo shook his head and stepped back, and Shawn advanced right with him.

"Hold it, Shawn."

Over Shawn's shoulder Fargo could see the marshal standing just within the door. Reflected light rippled along McClintock's trained gun barrel, and Shawn turned to face the lawman. McClintock said, "You can draw on me if you're anxious to fight."

Shawn shook his head. "Never quarrel with the drop. My

apologies, Marshal. I'll see you all later." He walked forward and tried to shoulder past McClintock.

McClintock gripped his shoulder and turned him back. "One minute, Shawn. There are a few things you ought to know."

"What's that?"

"For one, the circuit justice passed through this morning. He acquitted Stratemeier *in absentia*. That leaves you the number one suspect, friend, and it means if your boys do run Stratemeier down, you'll be an accessory to his murder. I would suggest you high-tail it home to call off your dogs. And I would also suggest that you'd serve your own best interests by riding far from this country in a very short time. When our citizens discover they've been duped, they're quite likely to run roughshod all over you, little friend. They've been itching to see you humbled ever since the day you rode in with your gun."

Shawn did not speak; there was a bright flame in his eyes. McClintock turned him gently by his small shoulder and gave him a slight push to propel him out of the restaurant. Before he left, the marshal allowed his glance to rest on Fargo. "If you're smart, you'll keep your nose so clean from here on in that a fly wouldn't touch it, bucko." And left.

Fargo used his sleeve to sweep beads of sweat from his forehead. Gracie had come to grip his sleeve, and now he put his arm around her; he could not keep her from feeling his trembling. He said, "Afraid one thing I'm short on is guts, Gracie."

She reached up and pulled his head down to meet her kiss.

CHAPTER SIXTEEN

Shawn fidgeted around his horse for the better part of his hour, irritably watching the mountain slopes and smoking cigars at a profound rate. Finally hoofbeats signaled from the near groves. He palmed his gun up and waited, and presently a voice issued from an unseen source: "Put the gun away, Shawn."

He nodded and holstered the gun. Boone Shields rode forth from the higher aspens, trailed by Naco on his pinto. Boone said, "What was the gun for?"

"I wasn't sure it was you."

"All right," Boone said.

Naco dropped lithely off the pinto. "Whatever you want us for, it better be pretty damned important."

"If it wasn't," Shawn said, "would I give you this kind of a chance at me?"

"You never know," Boone said.

"Get down, Boone. Let's talk."

Boone swung his bulk off the saddle. "Well?"

"I'm giving you your chance to become king of this country, Boone."

"I'm still listening," Boone said. He did not sound excited.

Shawn put his hands in his hip pockets and strode up and down. "Your grapevine's pretty good. I guess you already know Stratemeier's been acquitted."

"Sure enough," Boone said.

"But I've still got a fair-sized crew holding Hatchet."

"Uh-huh."

"Now, listen, Boone. When I moved a crew onto Hatchet, it was a bluff. I was just hoping they'd let me get away with it—and they did, for a while. But now they know Stratemeier's not a crook and Edith was lying. Which puts me strictly out in the cold. McClintock's getting set to run you and me out of the country, and Stratemeier's still banging around somewhere up in the hills."

"So what?" said Boone.

"Can't you smell the wind blowing through this country, Boone? It's a new breeze. You and I, we're behind the times. They won't allow us here."

"Hell," Boone said. "Stop cryin'. You've had your day, maybe, but mine ain't over yet by a long shot. It'll be a cold day in hell when McClintock pushes me out of War Pass."

"You're wrong, Boone."

Boone spat. "You've turned yellow, Shawn. You're spilling your guts all over the ground."

Shawn's eyes were bright when he turned to face Boone. "You listen to me, fat man. I've spent twenty years living by the gun, and the reason I'm still alive is I've always been smart enough to know when to move on. I'll tell you something. You run now, or you're dead."

"Hell, Shawn, you're scared to death—and you're trying to take me with you. War Pass has never been stronger. They couldn't take me with an army."

"But they could," Shawn said, "with a match. That town is tinder dry."

"Shawn, you can hide up in the hills for ten years and never be seen by a single human being. I know my own position—don't worry about that."

"Ah," Naco grunted. "He's loco, Boone. Let's fan our tails out of here."

Shawn held up his hands. "Wait. Hear me out."

"I will," Boone said, "if you say somethin'."

"What about Stratemeier?"

Boone's eyes snapped up in curiosity. "What about him? He's a fool."

"No. He thinks too fast. Mark me, Boone. McClintock and Stratemeier together are enough to run ten of you out of any stronghold in the world."

"He's too busy runnin' to stay alive," Boone said. "He won't bother us."

"A man gets pretty smart when he's thinking of his skin. And there's another thing, Boone. This will be the last time Hatchet will ever be as open to us as it is right now."

"What do you mean?"

Contempt quickened Shawn's glance. "Only a fool keeps panning when the pocket's cleaned out. There are ten thousand cattle on Hatchet. Yours and mine, if we take them. But we've got to watch McClintock and Stratemeier."

Boone was shaking his head. "You worry too much. We can lick the whole valley if we have to."

"You're a fool, Boone. Those people would fight like hell if they had time to organize."

"I've got fifty-three top guns at War Pass," Boone murmured. "And you must have seven or eight at Hatchet."

"Sure enough, Boone. Sure enough. Those gunnies love their own skins more than yours or mine, which is something you had best remember. If things get tough, they'll break—that's the nature of a crook every time."

"Ain't it," Naco agreed, displaying his sly perceptiveness. "Ain't it, now."

Boone said, "You've spent a lot of time goin' around the mulberry bush. Where's your point, Shawn?"

"You and I, Boone. We'll pool every rider we've got. We'll drive every head of Hatchet cattle out of the valley in one sweep—and never come back."

"I don't know," Boone said after a while. "I'll think on it."

"Good God! If I had just one man I could depend on to use his head once in a while—Do you need a set of blueprints, for God's sake?"

Boone's glance hit him with dry force. "What's worryin' you? Those cows will still be there tomorrow. I'll let you know. Come on, Naco."

Kathy McCune gaited across the bridge and up the Hatchet road with cold night air cutting through her blouse. When she was at the limit of earshot from the burned Hatchet layout, she paused, uncertain of what she was about to do. Shawn was full of cruelty and guile; she could only hope, she could not depend. She was about to put spurs to the pony's flanks when she was warned by the clattering messages of another horse coming across the bridge. She quickly wheeled through the night into the cover of a triangle of cottonwoods to wait for the oncoming horseman to pass.

It might have been Shawn himself; she wasn't sure. He rode into the yard and went up to the big tent that was serving as ranch house. When he pulled back the entrance flap, she recognized Shawn. She faced the tent and rode boldly into the yard. The sound of her arrival preceded her; when she dismounted, the flap once again opened. Shawn, lithe and confident, blocked the light for an instant and then moved out of it onto the packed earth. She advanced and halted beside the opening, feeling Shawn's eyes on her. A husky voice ripped forward from one of the far corrals behind her, startling her: "All right?"

"All right, Jubal." These were the first words Shawn had spoken, and the mildness of his tone surprised Kathy. He said, "What is it, Mrs. McCune?"

"I want to talk to you."

It was a feeling she received, the sardonic amusement coming from him. He went inside the tent and waited for her to follow, holding the tent flap back. A cool light reflected yellow out of his eyes; he showed his innate discontent, his antagonism and his bitterness. She began to speak, and was checked by the sudden sight of a woman standing somberly in a dim corner. The woman was slim and dark, and her face was hard. She put her unblinking eyes on Kathy and said not a word.

Shawn had stooped at the desk in the center of the tent to get a cigar. "Well?"

She looked around the interior of the tent, to the hard-looking woman silent in the corner. She looked like an Indian. Kathy said, "Does she have to be here?"

"She won't hurt you. You came because of Stratemeier, didn't you?"

"Yes."

Shawn spoke abruptly. "I wish my men had your guts. I'd be a lot more satisfied. You want me to leave Stratemeier alone—you're about to tell me that."

"Yes."

"Why did you expect me to listen to you?"

"There must be some kindness in you," she said. "What has he ever done to you?"

"That man will spend his dying breath cursing me, Mrs. McCune. My vocation for twenty years has consisted largely of making his life miserable. It may be I had no such personal intents and it may be I regret what has happened to Eric and to myself because of the obsession of a woman who is now dead. But the fact is I must protect myself—to stay alive myself I must prevent Eric from reaching me."

She shook her head. "He has never touched anything of yours."

"If he gets the chance, he'll kill me," Shawn said. "Eric is the only man I have ever feared, Mrs. McCune. I must stop him before he stops me."

"Oh, let him be!"

His lips moved, but a disturbance checked him—someone dismounting outside and coming forward in a considerable hurry. Naco burst in and spoke immediately, without seeing Kathy, who was behind him by the doorframe.

"Stratemeier was in town tonight, with McClintock. It's a wonder you didn't run into him. The two of them have arrested every one of our men in Antelope. Boone says he's with you on these cows, but let's round them up and get the hell out of here now."

Shawn was smiling, not otherwise visibly roused by the news. "All right, Naco. Ride up and tell Boone to get down here as soon as he can get his crew together." He turned to Kathy. "I'm afraid you've walked into it. I can't let you reach Stratemeier or McClintock with what you know now. You'll have to stay here until we're gone. Entana will take care of you."

Kathy looked at the Indian woman, then returned her glance to Shawn. "What then?"

"I'll let you go." He turned to the desk and crushed his cigar on its top. "Entana will put you up in the tack shed. I'll have men around the place—you're not to leave that building, understand?"

The Indian woman's eyes were hard and petulant. She tossed her head at Kathy. "Come on." She whirled outside, and after a moment Kathy followed her.

Ben Overmile was approaching the Ash bridge when two horsemen advanced from the cottonwoods beside the trail: Will Shawn and Naco. Shawn called, "Just a minute, Overmile."

Overmile reined in carefully. His hand rose to grip his gunbutt. Naco had a rifle balanced across his pommel, in a position to whip around at Overmile with a minimum of effort. Overmile said, "What is it, Shawn?"

"Let's keep this peaceful."

"I'm not shootin'. Not yet. What you want?"

Shawn's hands were crossed casually on the saddle horn. "I understand you've got some feeling for Mrs. McCune."

"What of it?"

"Just this. You find Stratemeier, Overmile, and tell him to keep himself and McClintock and the whole population right in Antelope for the next week."

"Why should I?"

"Because I've got Kathy McCune."

Overmile's knuckles tensed against the gunbutt; he leaned forward. "You let her loose, Shawn. If you like livin', you let her loose."

"In time," Shawn said evenly. "Tell that to Stratemeier. And tell him if he sets foot out of town within the next week, the same thing will happen to her that happened to his sister. Tell him that." He wheeled his horse and drummed north across the plain, with Naco following closely.

Overmile frowned. "Now what in hell was that supposed to mean?" And put his own horse down the Antelope road. His lips were pressed tight; color enriched his cheeks, and his spurs raked the pony's flank with urgency.

It was midafternoon when he tied up before the courthouse and went inside. Stratemeier sat on a corner of the dun-colored desk. Johnny Fargo sat morosely in a corner chair, and McClintock was peering through the dust-spattered window into the street. Overmile said, "I got a message. From Shawn. He's got Kathy. He told me to tell you to stay in town for a week if you don't want the same thing to happen to her that happened to your sister."

A cold gleam shone from Stratemeier's eyes, and for a moment Overmile thought Stratemeier was going to ram right through him. But Stratemeier's position did not change, and after a moment he nodded. Overmile said, "What you going to do?"

"Wait for nightfall," Stratemeier said. He rose and went outside.

Johnny Fargo tilted his chair back against the wall. "Well, now he knows. And I hope it doesn't kill him."

Overmile's attention swung to him. "Now he knows what?"

"A long time ago," Fargo murmured, "Stratemeier killed a man. The man was Edith Rachal's brother. Eric thought Rachal had raped his sister and killed her. But it wasn't Rachal. It was Shawn. So now he knows it."

"He knew it before," McClintock said mildly. "I hope Stratemeier gets to Kathy McCune before Videen gets to War Pass."

Overmile stood beside him. "How's that?"

"Haven't you been wondering where everybody is? Clay Videen's on his way to War Pass with better than a thousand miners in his posse. It seems Clay got impatient with the way I was working."

"What will happen?"

McClintock shrugged gently. "One of three things. The hill people will scatter and disappear into the hills, or they'll stand and fight, or they'll turn tail and run clear out of the country. You never know what they'll do. Clay's hoping they'll stand and fight. He likes to think of himself as a great general."

"He's likely to ruin the whole thing—he's likely to get Kathy killed! I'm going to get Stratemeier."

McClintock touched his arm. "Hold it. Don't you think he knows?"

Fargo said, "Will's probably got someone watching the town. If Eric rides out in daylight, that's all Will needs."

Overmile shook his head. "So he just sits and sweats."

"That's right," McClintock murmured. "That's the hardest thing of all, Ben. To sit and sweat. You leave him be."

"Sure," Overmile muttered. "But by God, if anything happens to Kathy—"

"Shut up," Fargo's voice was as mild as McClintock's. "Guess I'll go over to Gracie's," and stepped into the dusty street.

Overmile leaned against the window. His eyes were squinted and his head swung from side to side as his attention roved the quiet street. "Calm before the storm," he said. "I guess hell will pop soon enough."

"Sure enough," McClintock murmured. "I'd hate to be in Stratemeier's boots right now. That man's got his own strict code. Right now he's fighting it out with himself."

"Fighting what?"

"That kid he killed back twenty years ago. When you're a man like Stratemeier and you find out you've killed an innocent man, you don't breathe too easy."

"To hell with that," Overmile said. "He's paid for it plenty. That dead kid's sister made him pay over and over again for twenty years, and right now Shawn's making him pay more for it."

"You know that and I know that," McClintock said gently, "but it's going to take Stratemeier a while to know it."

CHAPTER SEVENTEEN

Boone Shields stood on the porch of his weathered saloon and spoke with a contemptuous voice: "A bunch of you take the horses and cache them up above the mine. The rest of you fort up along the street. Videen's going to lose a lot of lives if he wants to take this town. Now get a move on, damn it."

Without waiting for the mob of armed riders to obey, he turned into the saloon and slammed the door viciously behind him. Daylight filtered weakly through the spattered windows, revealing one man sitting calmly at a table with a bottle of rye by his hand. "Don't count on them," that man said. "They're sheep—they're scared and they'll run."

"I'll kill every man jack that hightails," Boone growled. "Maybe they're scared of Videen, but they're more scared of me."

"Don't count on it," the thin man murmured.

"Listen, Ringgold. You want to run, too?"

Ringgold smiled. "Not just yet. I want to see some of the fun first. Videen's got Milo Teague and Ross Thompson and Miles LeVane with him, and a thousand miners. You've got about forty hands here. The rest of your boys are halfway to Hatchet by now, and they won't be coming back just to save your skin. What do you think your forty scared jackrabbits can do against Videen's army?"

"Dirt-pickers," Boone growled. "Ain't a one of them ever handled a gun in his life. My boys are all sharp-shooters."

"Sure enough," Ringgold agreed. His long, handsome face was gently smiling.

"Ringgold," Boone said suddenly, "Get your tail out of that chair. Ride down to Hatchet and get my boys back. Bring Shawn's crew with you if you can."

Ringgold shrugged and rose from the table without hurry. "All right. But there's two things against it. First, they won't come, and second, if they would, I couldn't get them here before midnight. Videen'll probably ride in about sundown."

"Get going," Boone said. "Kill the horse if you have to."

Ringgold smiled and strode to the door. "So long, Boone."

When the door slammed Boone whirled to the bar, slammed his fist hard against its side, and walked with choppy strides to the door at the end of the bar. "Damn it to hell." In his office, he sat at his desk, staring through the window at the town that was his kingdom.

Around sundown he heard a short burst of shooting from the lower end of War Pass; the first skirmish had begun. Shields went to the heavy safe in the corner and opened it. Resting inside was a small carpetbag; he began to stuff it with banknotes and sacks of coins. When he had it full, he stared at it, not moving. Occasional shots sounded at closer intervals at the lower end of town. Shields' head shook back and forth; he closed the carpetbag, returned it to the safe, and closed the safe door. He went back to the desk and sat down slowly.

The door opened behind him. Boone turned his head slowly. Clay Videen stood spraddle-legged before Milo Teague and Miles LeVane and a small group of men. Shields' face was mild. "What do you men want here?"

"You," Videen said. A miner came up to stand by him with a knotted rope in his fist. The crowd rumbled.

"It was a good game," Shields murmured.

"While it lasted," Milo Teague answered.

"Yeah," Shields breathed. "While it lasted. Listen, Shawn won't get away, will he?"

"Not a chance," Clay Videen said. "Don't worry about it, Shields."

"No," Shields whispered. "No. You know, Shawn thinks he can outrun it. But it'll root and grow in him. Munguia and Charley Sharpe and that Rachal woman—they'll outlive us all. You know that?"

Videen stepped to the side of the doorway. "Let's go, Shields."

Shields looked at him quietly, then stepped into the barroom. He did not fight against the hands thrusting him forward. The street was filled with a mob of miners riding horses and mules, hefting rifles and shotguns. "Come on," Videen said. "We'll find a tree."

Milo Teague said, "I guess this is trial, conviction, and execution, Boone. Was it worth it?"

"Why," Boone said, "I guess I'll never know that, Milo. By the way, there's a bunch of your horses at Hector Valenzuela's in Kingman."

"Thanks," Teague said. The mob rumbled; Shields felt himself pressed forward by its mass, moving steadily toward the head of the street. Above a caved-in house stood a venerable oak. Ross Thompson tested the knot in the rope and slung it over a limb. He tied the free end to the trunk. Nelson Satterlee, Antelope's storekeeper, led a horse forward through the mob.

"Mount up," Videen said.

Shields glanced darkly at the crowd, climbed on the saddle, and looked down at Videen. Ross Thompson slipped off his belt and tied Shields' hands behind him with it. Videen stood on tiptoe, slipped the noose over Shields' head, and fixed the knot just behind his left ear.

Milo Teague said, "Want to make a speech, Boone?"

"Well, yes, I guess I do. I guess from here on I'll sleep better than any of you boys here. It was fun while it lasted. Clay, I'll meet her go, Milo."

Teague took off his hat and slapped the horse violently with it. The horse bolted and ran awkwardly down into town, stirrups flapping and tail flying. At the last moment Shields sprang high in the air, and came down hard against the noose. His neck broke with an audible snap.

There was silence in the mob. One voice broke through: "Why didn't he run with the rest of them?"

"He was the captain of his ship."

"Well," said Ross Thompson, "somebody climb up there and cut him down."

Stratemeier dismounted, removed his boots and hung them on the saddle, and moved forward in his socks, threading the darkness of the cottonwood grove and coming to a cautious halt beside a thick paloverde at the edge of the plain.

The lights of Hatchet winked across the plain; men's voices rose from the yard in wisps of sound. The scene was dim and ghostly. Stratemeier started off downslope, moving bent half over, his fingertips almost touching the ground. Kathy might be bait for Shawn's trap, but tonight Strate-

meier had no other choice, with Videen on the march to
War Pass.

Twenty yards from the first corral he achieved the cover
of a manzanita bush without attracting attention from the
yard. He paused here, his gun in his fist, and considered
the activity at the headquarters. Men went to and from one
large tent near the center of things at quick intervals, and
once Stratemeier saw Shawn's bantam silhouette in its
entranceway. Once also he saw the figure of a dark-haired
woman in that tent, but careful study of her figure and the
way she moved assured him it was not Kathy. Action was
busy around the corrals, where horses were being saddled
and tied. Shawn must be preparing to move, though
Stratemeier did not know what direction that move would
take. A group of riders arrived from the northeast, probably
coming in off a nightherd shift, and dismounted before the
main tent. One of them went inside, perhaps making a
report. The woman left the main tent and traveled across
the edge of the yard to another wide tent that had smoke
rising from apertures in its roof. Presently she reappeared
with a tray and quartered to the tack shed, unlocked the
door, placed the tray inside, shut the door again, and
walked back toward the main tent.

There was one short area in the woman's path of travel
that Stratemeier put his attention on—a small grove of
cottonwoods where her figure disappeared for a number of
seconds, then reappeared on the nearer edge of camp. And
when the woman entered the main tent, Stratemeier noted
her varicolored cotton dress.

He remained by his post for another moment and then
retreated from the manzanita, moving back almost to the
edge of the cottonwoods before he turned northeast and
began circling the camp. It took him quite a while to
achieve the cottonwood grove by the razed bunkhouse;
activity was heavy around the yard, and it was difficult to
avoid the paths of aimlessly moving men. Presently he was
crouched by the bole of the heaviest of the cottonwoods. In
his pocket he found a sheet of paper and the stub of a
pencil. He wrote a brief note, then squatted back by the
tree, waiting.

A rider came drumming up from the river, whirled into
camp, and dismounted by the tent. Will Shawn appeared
from inside; he looked lean and angry, his cheeks had

turned gaunt. The horseman just arrived stepped down and when he walked into the light, Stratemeier recognized him from the past—Otto Ringgold, whose gun was always for hire.

Shawn spoke with the gunfighter, swung on his heels, and lifted his voice above the camp's murmur: "Everybody up here—let's go. On the run."

Time stretched slowly while the group of riders at the corral moved forward and a dozen other men filed on foot into the center of activity. They formed a tight little group milling about apprehensively without direction until Shawn stepped back to the open front of his tent and lifted an arm for silence.

Shawn's pose reflected his arrogance. "Each one of you rope out the best horse you've got. Check your guns and load anything you want to keep on your saddles. We're getting out tonight, and we won't be coming back. Boone Shields is washed up. Videen took an army up there, and by now War Pass is strictly a ghost town. But while Videen's up there banging around in the mountains, we're going to be driving every head of cattle on Hatchet west over the mountains. If any man gets in your way, shoot him down. Now get saddled."

The crew split up and drifted away from the yard, and Shawn turned with an abrupt twist of his little body and disappeared inside the tent. Within a few moments the dark-haired woman appeared in its entrance and walked listlessly forward. Stratemeier stood and put himself behind the bole of the tree. The woman's moccasined footsteps approached steadily, and when she was immediately before the tree Stratemeier said softly, "Hold it, woman. My gun is on you."

She stopped. Stratemeier spoke again, without coming from the shadows. "There's a note at your feet. Pick it up."

The woman bent and grasped the pale sheet of paper, and straightened. Stratemeier said, "Give that to the woman in the shed. Do what she tells you. Only one woman will come out of that door, and if it is the wrong one I'll pull the trigger. Understand?"

Her voice was quite calm. "Yes." She waited a moment more, and when he did not speak, she swung her foot forward and headed on toward the tack shed. She bent over the lock and swung the door open, and disappeared inside.

The door closed behind her. Across by the corrals, men were leading saddled horses out one by one and joining the ranked line of waiting riders. Shawn came out of the big tent with a carpetbag. He lit a cigar and stuck it in a corner of his mouth. Beside him, Ringgold said something and removed his hat to look at the sky. Shawn turned, frowning, facing the tack shed, and took several steps in that direction. Stratemeier's gun rose, but then Shawn shook his head and turned back.

The tack shed door swung open. In the doorway stood a dark-haired woman wearing a cotton print dress, carrying a tray of empty plates. She stepped down from the doorway, faced the door and set the lock, and turned to bring the tray forward, walking quite slowly. Stratemeier stood flat against the tree, his attention whipping from the advancing woman to Shawn and back. Shawn glanced at her once, then touched Ringgold's shoulder and walked toward the corral, leading his horse. Shawn mounted and spoke curtly, dividing his men up into groups and giving his orders. The woman came on. When she was abreast Stratemeier murmured: "Over here. Don't move fast."

She turned and rounded the tree; she set the tray on the ground and rose to press herself against him. He felt the trembling of her body and the pressure of her hands against his back. She said, "You shouldn't have come." Her lips sought his hungrily.

"Come on," he said. "Take it slow and quiet."

Stratemeier sat his horse, silent in the aspens, and watched the moon set. He listened against the wind for a moment, gently sliding by, and with that precaution taken, pulled out his pipe and lit it. He pulled a few puffs from it and blew rings in the air; he held the pipe in his cupped palm and looked into the glowing bowl. A single rider rolled up from the meadow, and Stratemeier's voice cut forward harshly: "Morg?"

"Nobody else." McClintock came on up and posted himself beside Stratemeier. "Been waiting for this," the marshal said. "It's been a while coming."

"About twenty years," Stratemeier murmured.

"It started a million years ago, sir. In Paradise. This is part of the same game that men will be playing at until they disappear from the face of the earth. It never changes."

McClintock's voice was carefully muted. "It may be that Shawn has been riding for a fall and that tonight it will come. But don't get reckless. Shawn thinks he's the man who'll write your ticket, and he may be if you give him enough of a chance."

"My ticket was written long before Will Shawn was born."

McClintock said, "Kathy's roosting at the hotel. I believe you pulled her out of that just in time. Shawn wouldn't have taken her with him, and if he'd left her behind, he wouldn't have left her alive."

"You can't tell what he would have done," Stratemeier said.

The moon had gone down. There was a faint purple in the eastern sky. McClintock said, "Someone's coming—heads up."

Drumming rose in the night and grew louder, and died abruptly when the advancing riders hit the mossy, neddle-carpeted floor of the timber district higher up. Stratemeier drew his Remington and held it against his thigh. The horsemen descended into the aspens and rolled forward. John Fargo's voice called softly from the night: "Eric?"

"Here."

They came in, a tight bunched group, and sat uneasily clustered around McClintock and Stratemeier. McClintock said, "Where are they?"

"They'll be along directly," Ben Overmile said. Stratemeier's glance peered carefully through the dark and he recognized Fargo's men, Anse Sheffield and Lee Rawls, in the little group behind Fargo and Overmile. Seven or eight other men crowded close, faces he had seen in Antelope. Morgan McClintock sat back, crooking a leg around the saddle horn. Juan Soto of the old Hatchet crew carried an old .50 caliber Spencer rimfire across the saddle before him. Silence became pregnant; tension reached out to inject restlessness into the horses, enough to make them mill on the muffling forest carpet. Stratemeier hit his saddle horn softly with his fist. Morgan McClintock wore an unperturbed calmness about him.

"And the meek," Ben Overmile murmured, "shall get their pants shot off." Stratemeier could feel the force of Overmile's driving impatience. It seemed to touch them all.

In the vague light Johnny Fargo's face was long and flat; it held no trace of anxiety.

The first sound of distantly drumming hoofs began to reach their ears—horses and cattle together, coming down out of the plains to the east and south. "They're headed here," Overmile said. "I was right—they'll gather them in this valley before they push them on."

Hatchet—the new Hatchet—came with the first dim rays. Two dozen riders, short and tall, thin and squat, from Texas and Wyoming, from Illinois and Mexico. They drove a herd of six thousand cattle before them, the men's scattered silhouettes rising over the humping sea of cattle.

McClintock lost his slouch. His drone barely reached Stratemeier: "We'll split up. They've got us two to one, so we've got to make surprise add up for us. Work around through the trees and circle them. Nobody shoots until I call out. Nobody. Now move."

Stratemeier moved out, threading the trees, moving southeast along the fringe of timber. He had to pull up and wait almost half an hour while Shawn's crew pushed the herd past him into the grass bowl. Dawn was becoming brighter. Stratemeier crossed the path behind the herd's drag to get around on the farther flank. The gunmen were moving the stock silently; there was no whooping, no swirling ropes, no calls. Stratemeier reined in at the edge of the inner trees and watched Shawn's men moving through the herd, bunching the cattle. When he concentrated his attention, he could recognize Shawn in there and thought he marked the squat figure of Naco. One voice spoke low, sounding like Otto Ringgold. Morgan McClintock threw his call forward from the opposite timber, firm and unhurried:

"Throw up your hands. You're boxed—we've got you cold."

CHAPTER EIGHTEEN

A wave of shock rippled through the Hatchet horsemen. One rider, in the meadow near Stratemeier, cursed at great volume and roweled his pony. He was making for the timber close by Stratemeier, whipping his gun up and shooting wildly over his shoulder in the direction of McClintock's voice. Then they were all shooting. Stratemeier lifted his gun and centered it on the oncoming rider's chest. "Pull up, Ringgold—pull up!"

He couldn't tell whether the gunman heard him in the rising din. Ringgold's revolver swung forward and Stratemeier pulled off an initial shot that was too hasty. The bullet went a few inches wide. He pulled the Remington down and squeezed off a single shot that spun Ringgold to the ground. Ringgold's horse ran by in panic, stirrups bouncing against its flanks. Stratemeier looked down at the dead man, then sent his horse down into the meadow.

A figure loomed abruptly—Will Shawn. "Stratemeier! Damn you, Stratemeier—" And suddenly the tide of aimlessly stampeding cattle changed, and Shawn was washed away with them, in a new direction into the dimness of forest shadows. Stratemeier lost sight of him as suddenly as he had seen Shawn; it seemed a scene out of a nightmare. A horseman rushed forward, lifting a shotgun; Stratemeier pumped two bullets into him and watched the man spill to the ground, wretched regret clouding his face. Stratemeier ran on through the thundering half-night. Gunshots were loud in the dawn, throwing out long, bright glaring flashes.

Somewhere behind him a high, strident yell went up. Stratemeier's pistol swung, but he held fire. Ben Overmile rushed forward. He waved his gun and pounded on into the melee. Stratemeier put his horse after Overmile, toward the main body of the fight at the lower end of the meadow. He heard the boom of Juan Soto's big .50 caliber Spencer opening up from the trees down there; riders milled wildly, and confusion made the scene grotesque. Suddenly Stratemeier saw Overmile's arms thrown up; Overmile tilted backward and cried out and fell over the horse's rump to the ground. Cattle milled around him, and Stratemeier lost sight of him; he put his horse urgently through the steers and swung down beside Overmile, prone on the dew-damp ground. But Overmile brought up a single bubbling grin, and died. When Stratemeier swung back into the saddle, he emptied the Remington savagely at the winking gun flashes.

The breaking day was a swirling, rushing mass of crying and explosion, half-light disrupted by the constant flaming of black powder. Urgency and rash anger were spoiling Stratemeier's aim, and in the confusion he knew his bullets were not reaching targets. A steer whirled crazily by with half its face torn off by a shotgun charge. Down below, groups of men swung together and apart, and then, suddenly, the riot ended, as an abrupt intake of breath. Silence descended, a heavy blanket, disturbed only by the lowing of the few bunches of Hatchet cattle that had not stampeded out of the bowl. There was a single ragged after-volley. Stratemeier heard the drum of horses rushing away and a voice calling from the north end of the field: "Eric—Eric! Where in hell is everybody?"

He rode toward the voice. The moon had slid over a cloud again and darkness was close around him. Sudden mounted shapes loomed, and he spoke quickly:

"Who's that—who's that?"

"Fargo."

A match flared and soon died, but by its brief light Stratemeier saw a man lying on the grass in the complete shadow of a cottonwood. "Who's down?"

"Juan Soto."

"Juan," Stratemeier said, "you hurt?" There was a period of quiet while they all waited to hear an answer.

"I am." When Soto's voice finally came it was cracked and weak in his throat. "I think I'm hit in the leg."

Stratemeier stepped down to kneel by the prone figure of the cowboy. "Not too bad," he said, and heard the release of Soto's breath. Behind him he heard the whirling of a horse and the pound of hoofs and McClintock's voice:

"Where you going?"

Stratemeier wheeled and heard John Fargo's one-word reply: "Naco."

Stratemeier said, "What's that?"

"They stole a lot of money from Fargo," McClintock said. "Naco's got it on his saddle. He lit out when the lead started to fly."

Stratemeier rose and went back to his horse. He lifted his left hand to the sorrel's withers. "Who's here?"

"McClintock," the marshal said.

"Sheffield."

"I'm still here," Juan Soto said dryly.

"Rawls."

Half a dozen men called their names. Stratemeier said, "I saw Overmile go down back there. He's dead. Anyone else?"

Lee Rawls said, "Jeremy Mossgrove cashed in up in the aspens. And I sent Tom Brand back to town. He had a busted wing."

Stratemeier swung up slowly to the saddle. "How about Shawn's crew?"

"I buffaloed one over the head back there," McClintock said. "He'll keep until I pick him up. I had to shoot three men. Two of them may be dead."

Stratemeier said, "Ringgold's down. I spotted Shawn once, but lost him. Anyone see him?"

"He was runnin' south," someone said. "That was a while ago."

McClintock stepped down to give Juan Soto a hand to his horse. "I suppose most of the ones that got away with whole skins will keep running for quite a way. Come on, Juan. Stratemeier—where you headed?"

"Shawn," Stratemeier said. He put his horse to a run and swept away.

The world had fallen in, and Will Shawn was at the bottom of a profound pit. He let his mind run back over the battle as he rode the trail to the Ash.

The cook wagon waited silently by the river ford. Shawn reached into it and brought out his heavy carpetbag and slung it on his saddle, then yanked the horse around and splashed through the river and straight into the mountains.

It started raining above the foothills, and the weather slowed him. It was well after noon when he reached War

Pass in the wake of the storm and circled to the back side of a small house at the near end of town, a shack built long ago by a prospector, abandoned to decay.

So much was sure, Stratemeier would let no grass grow under his boots before he came on. Shawn's crowd was broken up; he had no way of estimating how many were dead, and did not wish to guess; and regardless of the damage, those who had escaped were undoubtedly halfway to Colorado.

"It wasn't in the stars," he said. He went to the shack's door to look up the street at the empty town, shaking his head, not understanding.

He looked at himself furtively; he shouted at the vacant town: "Damn this world for not giving me what's mine!" The curse kept running through his mind like the clack-clack of railroad wheels on a track.

He should raid the town for supplies and fade out of this country, but he could not. Stratemeier would follow him to the end of time. He must stand.

With the sun hardly an hour high, Naco rode his hard breathing pinto into Antelope. He rammed through the streets and pulled up before the Pioneer House in a sudden cloud of risen sand. Without touching the ground, he leaped from the wind-broken pinto's back to the saddle of a long-legged dun gelding standing hipshot by the rack. He leaned forward to gather the reins and quirted it into an immediate gallop. Behind him, a cowboy ran out on the boardwalk and howled after him: "Where you goin' with my horse? Hey—hey!"

It was not much more than half an hour later that Johnny Fargo cantered down the street. He saw Naco's horse and listened to the owner of the stolen pony, then left town immediately on Naco's trail. When he came to a fork he made his guess. Naco was an unimaginative man in a hurry to quit the country. Naco would take the shortest trail to the railroad at Seligman. Fargo put his horse onto the road leading south-southwest.

It was a good fifty-five-mile ride to Seligman. Well after sundown Fargo passed the junction to the road to Red Lake, a bit past the halfway point. The horse was not keeping a good pace, and Fargo dared not push it faster than a trot; urgency put fright into him and he chafed until he came past Aubrey's ranch, and turned in. "Hey, the house!"

Aubrey came to the window, white-haired and bearded, holding a lamp beside his head. "What in hell is eatin' you at this hour?"

"I'm chasing a killer," Fargo said. "My horse is played out. I've got to take one of yours. I'll leave it on the way back."

Aubrey grunted testily. "All right, all right—go ahead. But be quiet about it."

Fargo roped out a deep-chested blue roan from the corral, threw his saddle on, leaped aboard, and raced out of the yard at a high gallop. The moon was up and bright enough to guide him along the humping road. The powerful blue ran with a mile-eating length in its stride. Early in the morning hours he sighted the peak of Mount Floyd to his left, an eight-thousand-foot black guardian of the high plateau. He splashed twice through the double bend of Chino Creek. In his mind rode the picture of Naco's saddlebags heavy with the fortune Syl Hollister had stolen from him that night along the Ash. There was with it in his mind a picture of Gracie and a picture of the peaceful life he could have only by regaining the coin that Naco's gun guarded.

There was a clock on Otero's store in Seligman: seven o'clock when Fargo rode down the wide street, past scattered adobes and frame fronts on to the AT&SF depot. A Negro roustabout was sweeping dust from the porch. Fargo put a harsh-voice question to him: "Any train gone out yet this morning?"

The boy shook his head. "One due in half an hour."

"Thanks," Fargo said. He led the horse around and finally let it at the water trough, then hitched it to a rail before the depot. No one was on the street aside from a group of worshipers leaving the church at the head of the street. He mounted the platform and walked inside the station, his hand warily rising to the holster. One man, a drummer probably, sat across the room; otherwise it was deserted. Fargo shook his shoulders and sat down on the hard wooden bench.

He had made his guess. If it was wrong, Naco would be a hundred miles away from here. Fargo pressed a hand against his forehead to compress the sweat of nerves. He told himself there was no hurry. If Naco was here at all, he was probably keeping hidden, waiting until just before the train pulled out to show himself. Fargo withdrew a cheroot from his pocket; he puffed on it and let his eyes trace the grain in the floorboards. He looked at the clock above the ticket cage: seven-ten.

At eight-twenty he went to the window and looked out across the depot platform. Nothing stirred. Wind roughed up the leaves of a lone cottonwood by the depot corner. Once he heard a sound behind him and whirled; the Negro boy gave him a curious, wide-eyed look and walked past him to the door. Fargo turned his attention back to the street.

The train whistle signaled dismally down the track. Fargo started. It seemed a signal for the town. The wide doors of the livery stable swung open, and a yawning man in overalls came out on the saloon porch down the street to slop water out of a bucket onto the porch. And a stocky figure appeared behind that man in the saloon doorway. Fargo thought, *Now's the time*. The figure stepped off the walk by the saloon and quartered forward.

The window stood open by Fargo's cheek; he lifted his gun out of the holster. But then Naco stopped. His left hand was burdened with a pair of full saddlebags; his right hand stopped swinging and hung by his holstered gun.

Naco had seen him. A tear rolled out of the corner of Fargo's eye and dampened his dusty cheek. And somewhere out of the far past a voice called to him: "You're a man, Fargo. Prove it."

"Prove it." He spoke aloud and holstered his gun and walked to the door. When he reached for the knob his hand paused. *Prove it*.

He opened the door and swung onto the platform. On the edge of the boards he halted, eyes narrowed, to watch Naco. He wiped his palm on his chest.

He stepped off and walked twenty feet out into the dusty road. The lobe of his left ear itched. He stood firm, legs braced wide apart.

Naco's grin slid into place across his lips, and his hand rose to hang over his gun. Naco said, "Step out of the way, dude." His legs began to move; he walked steadily, his grin frozen.

"I'll step aside," Fargo said, "if you'll drop those saddlebags and walk away from them."

There was no humor in Naco's grin. He spoke softly: "So
long, dude." His hand dropped and contracted around the
revolver's handle.

Fargo leaped sideways. He fell and rolled, pulling his
gun out. He lay on his stomach, the gun out before him,
and watched Naco's pistol coming up. He saw Naco's thumb
earing the hammer back and he thought, *Prove it,* and
pulled the trigger.

He knew before he heard the shot that he had missed.
Naco fired, and Fargo felt the jolt of it, he felt the sudden
numbness and warmth. He thought, *What a shame. What a
damned, crying shame.* Naco was still walking forward,
cocking his gun for another shot. Fargo's vision blurred.
Everything was happening so slowly. Tears got into his eyes;
he blinked; a scream tore from his throat: "Prove it! Prove
it!"

He let his shot off, holding the gun in both hands.

Naco dropped the gun. His hands rose, fluttered. His
eyes bulged, and he buckled at the knees. He cried, he fell;
he raised a little whorl of dust, and was still.

Fargo's arms dropped to the ground. He closed his eyes
and lowered his head to rest it. He knew he would never lift
it again, and the silent tears washed his cheeks.

CHAPTER NINETEEN

Stratemeier had his look around Hatchet headquarters and satisfied himself that Shawn had not been here. He remounted his pony, turned out of the yard, and ran down toward the bridge. Flagrant echoes rose in the dark; a hail lifted and brought him up short: "Stratemeier!" He waited with some suspicion for the following rider to catch up.

It was McClintock. The marshal advanced quickly and said, "Tracks all over the place. Someone's around here, or been here recently."

"I don't think so," Stratemeier said. "Fargo chased Naco past here, and some of Shawn's bunch probably ran through this way. My guess is Shawn headed for the mountains."

"Think he'll run on through?"

"No. Shawn will get no rest until he sees me dead. He'll wait for me, maybe at War Pass."

"Maybe," McClintock said. "And so you're going after him with a gun."

"That's it."

"Well, it's a nice morning. I guess I'll just ride along."

Toward noon, well above Bear Creek Pass and just beyond Maldonado's empty shack, the two riders came upon a freshly broken trail in the damp ground. Stratemeier said, "He's leaving tracks a blind man could follow."

"Not trying to hide. But he could be waiting anywhere. I'd suggest we don't go into this with a lot of slack in our triggers."

"Good advice," Stratemeier said.

"Not over an hour old, the tracks."

"We won't catch him this side of War Pass."

"We might," McClintock said cryptically, and gave fuller attention to the surrounding trees. "We might."

They traveled steadily higher until they crossed a gravel ford in a creek running swiftly down the mountain's flank. McClintock said, "Best get off the road here," and turned into the trees, not intending to use the road again.

Presently they entered the deep-cut gorge that, a distance further on, enclosed War Pass. Riding through the cut, they divided, each man riding close along one wall of the gorge, warily searching the curves and juts ahead, any of which could conceal a marksman. They circled and came toward town from the west, by the tidings slope at the head of the gulch; they moved crouched, well away from each other, senses filed sharp and guns ready.

McClintock paused and held up his hand for caution. In a shed below, open to the front, a single man stood engrossed in skinning out a dead steer. McClintock murmured: "Guess a few of them decided the town's cooled off enough to move back in. That's Charlie Caldwell."

At that instant Caldwell flung a startled glance at them and retreated to the shadowed interior of the shed. In a moment he reappeared by its corner, lifting a pistol; he fired once, and ran around the side of the building to disappear into town.

Will Shawn heard the shot. "They're on me fast." He ran out of the shack he had paused in, went down behind the town on the east side, and stopped behind Shields' saloon. After listening a moment at the back door, he stepped in, closed the door tight, and swung to face the two shabby occupants of the place. "What was that shot?"

"I don't know," the first man, Stuart, said. "Hey, Wallace—ain't Caldwell up the gulch somewhere?"

"I guess so," Wallace said. Then to Shawn: "What happened to you?"

"My boys are scattered from hell to breakfast," Shawn said. "McClintock ambushed us on Hatchet."

"Tough," Stuart said blandly. He shot his undimmed hostility at Shawn. Since the night Shawn had run from this saloon, none of the hill people had shown him any sympathy.

"I need some help," Shawn said. "If you boys want to keep this town for yourselves, you'll ride with me. I want to wipe Stratemeier and McClintock off the map."

"Tall order," Wallace said.

Stuart swung his back to the bar and put his elbows on it, his hands hanging limp by his waist. "Shawn, you'll get no help here. Fight your own fight."

Shawn was scowling, but then he shrugged. The two men stared narrowly at him; he went to the back door and whirled outside, suddenly afraid.

He paused in the alley to search both ends, and snarled. Nothing stirred within sight. He walked into the stable behind the saloon. An Indian pony, half Appeloosa, stood hipshot in a stall. Shawn hauled a saddle off a rack and flung it across the horse's back and tightened the cinch. He took the rope halter off the horse's dappled head and bridled it. "I'll get away—I'll kill Eric—I'll kill all of them." He heard sounds from the saloon—someone spoke loudly and boots clumped across the floorboards. Shawn's lips curled back from his teeth. He heard his own giggle.

A man moved along the alley, walking lightly, and Shawn stepped farther back into the stable. The man paused in the doorway to search the dark interior. No light fell on the man's face; Shawn could not recognize him, but knew it was not Stratemeier. He stood wholly still in the shadows until the searcher whirled down the alley out of sight. *Was that McClintock? He's with Stratemeier—they must have a crowd up here. No matter—I'll cut every man down.* Across the alley he saw the back door to the saloon open. Wallace and Stuart stood within it, looking up and down the drizzling alley, their collars turned up and their hats turned down and their faces a gray-blue like the rain itself. But then someone spoke behind them and they turned back into the saloon, shutting the door. Shawn pulled the saddle cinch tight and led the pony softly forward toward the doors. He had a careful look both ways along the alley. *I've got enough bullets for every man.* Abruptly, he swung into the saddle and broke the horse into a gallop through the mud of the narrow alley.

Suddenly Stratemeier was ahead of him. The man must have materialized out of the mud ooze itself. "Stop there, Will—stand fast!"

He threw a shot at Stratemeier, fought the horse around, and roweled toward the far end of the alley. He turned in his seat to fire again. Stratemeier answered the shot. Shawn's horse faltered, and he knew the animal was hit. "Damn, damn, why didn't I run him down? Oh, God!" He leaped hard sideways from the saddle and run afoot for the cover of a building alongside. Stratemeier was standing wide-footed in the middle of the alley, sending another shot searching after him.

Shawn felt tears in his eyes. *Damn you! Damn you all!*

The light was poor for shooting. Stratemeier missed his third shot, and then Shawn had disappeared beyond the corner. Stratemeier ran down the alley past the length of the building and turned the corner sharply, body braced, gun up. A shadow weaved at the far end and disappeared. Stratemeier ran forward along the side of the shack. Mud spattered his boots and trouser legs. When he stopped at the corner, he had lost all sound and sight of Shawn. He paused to try to guess Shawn's next move. The man might be circling the building to come up behind him. He turned a half-circle on his heels and backtracked.

But his guess was wrong. Nothing stirred. He was alone in the open with Shawn. Those few others in the town watched and waited silently while the two of them crept about, each man trying to maneuver the other into a trap. It was a morbid, tortuous game that McClintock was judiciously staying out of, doing his part by keeping the other residents of the town pinned down to give Stratemeier an open battleground.

Stratemeier retraced his path into the alley, and seeing nothing, walked slowly back to the rear of the saloon. He still had seen nothing move when he arrived at the space between the saloon and the stable. The waiting bothered him; he wanted to get it over with. He turned into the back door of the saloon and walked straight forward. When he came in, one of the two men at the bar gave him a glance full of hatred. McClintock stood by the front door, squinting into the gray street. "You lost him?"

"I got his horse. He's around somewhere."

McClintock nodded. He went around the bar and poured a short drink. Stratemeier fastened his gaze narrowly on the two drifters by the bar, and both of them slowly lifted their hands and placed them carefully, palms down, on the bar.

One of the men spoke mildly: "What's the matter—got a sore corn?"

Stratemeier walked to the front door, had his look through, and stepped outside. He put his whole attention on the street before him and the row of shacks across the mud. Shawn could be waiting in any of those. Stratemeier crossed the wide road openly and circled behind the end building, looking down the alleys as he walked boldly past them. At the end of the row, he had neither seen nor heard any sign. He turned back to begin a methodical search of each building.

Behind the first shack, its door long since fallen away, the smell of abandonment came out at him, musty and damp. He looked in carefully. Corners were black and shadowed. The town and the building were silent, waiting.

The next shack had burlap over the windows, dirty and rotting, admitting almost no light. It might be the place. He stepped inside and paused out of the doorway light, catching sign of nothing. He set one foot before him, testing the floor, letting his weight press down slowly, and then tried the other foot. He discovered the place had no floor, only packed earth. Coolness ruffled the back of his neck. He whirled. Nothing. Satisfied, he went out again to the back of the old jail, built here in the days of lusty miners. He made his search thorough and went on. It went that way, structure to structure; when he was through, he had found nothing in this half of the town. He crossed the street to the saloon again and circled it; he stood for a moment at the end of the alley, running the length of the pass. He waited another moment between the saloon's back door and the mouth of the stable.

That was when he heard movement. It could be a horse in the stable, but he made a bluff. "Will."

He called and immediately swung inside the stable and whirled aside from the doorway to get out of the light.

No sign. He said, "Will, I came to take you back to Antelope. I guess you won't want that. So let's finish it. Come out in the open."

"This will do." Shawn's voice came from deep within. Stratemeier put all his concentration on the back portion of the stable. A light scratch sounded. He placed the man somewhere on his own side of the building, close to the rear.

He laid his glance on that area and held it there, remaining just inside and just beside the doorway. Patience held him; he stood fast. As he waited he remembered Janice and Edith and Warren, and himself as he once had been. He stood utterly still, knowing that in time Shawn's nerves would react. The silence dragged into minutes, and at last Stratemeier heard a hard, sighing breath. Shawn's gun opened up and raked the corner of the stable with a reckless burst. Stratemeier heard one bullet *thwack* against something alive—he heard a horse stumble and thrash the wall, and drop against the stall.

Shawn had fired four shots. He had one, possibly two, left.

"You wasted those, Will. I'm coming in." He moved forward softly. The back door, straight ahead, was half open, gray against black. He crawled past the dead horse and halted within the stall next to it. He slid into the stall and called: "Right here, Will."

For a moment Shawn did not move. Then Stratemeier heard the scrape of his motion along a wall, and hearing it, lifted his gun and fixed the sights on the lighter dimness of the back door, hoping Shawn would cross that light. Stratemeier cocked the Remington loudly; the sound again might disturb Shawn. It did. Shawn took shape against the rear opening. Stratemeier stepped out of the stall, into the center of the front runway, deliberately putting himself in the door's light. "We're even—Right here, Will."

Shawn fired. Stratemeier answered, and Shawn stumbled, fell to his knees. Stratemeier said, "Want more, Will?" He walked slowly toward the man, the long-barreled Remington hanging the length of his arm. When Shawn lifted his gun Stratemeier pulled his own trigger again.

Shawn's gun exploded into the floor and flew out of his hand in recoil. He leaned forward on his knees and toppled face down into the ground, his face turned to the side. He suddenly grinned and whispered, "Who gives a damn?"

He clutched his chest, and died. The echoes of gunfire rebounded through the town.

The sky was bleak when Stratemeier crossed the alley into the saloon. He gave McClintock and the other three men—Caldwell must have come down from the shed—a single short glance and got a bottle from the back-bar. He took one stiff swallow. "You people are all through up here. You'll find Shawn dead out in the stable. After you've buried him, ride over the hill. The next time I come up here, I'll hang any man still here and burn the town. Now get out."

Caldwell and the two drifters stood away from the bar

and cruised to the back door, not visibly ruffled, and went out.

McClintock said, "I don't know where your strength comes from. I'm dead beat. All done?"

"All done." He blew out the lamp. They walked with sure strides to the upper end of town, climbed on their horses and rode through the deserted street.

CHAPTER TWENTY

There was a reporter in town, from one of the Chicago dailies, come to cover the Ash Valley war as one of the many sensational scenes of the Western play that received constant prominence on Eastern pages of pulp. The town was reeling from the sweeping climax that had put a sudden end to the bitter years, just as a man would reel from an unexpected blow delivered to his belly. Miners and cowboys alike made of it a holiday. It was a comment on the alertness of men that very few of them wore arms today. Lee Rawls and his fellow gentlemen of the trade spoke in precise, tuneless voices, presiding over men restless to face risk. Gracie Peters' restaurant was closed; word had come of Fargo's death. But to the town it did not matter today that the Pioneer House was without an owner, or that tomorrow would see the cemetery's population swelled as no single day in history had swelled it.

Up the valley road, a single rider trotted by the river. And farther on, ashes marked the ruins of Hatchet, gray in a rain as dismal as the very downpour of twenty years past at Vicksburg. By the corrals two men soberly regarded each other across ten feet of space. Morgan McClintock seemed to choose his words with great care. "Sir, it has been an honor to fight with you. A man in my situation can afford few friends. I have chosen a life that requires my becoming more of a legend than a man. And there are few men alive that a legend can trust."

"What now?" Stratemeier said.

"My guns," McClintock said, "are my life. I will be moving on, to find another town where they are needed. There is always another town, sir. You're a man to ride the river with. I hope we meet again." His squat, powerful frame rose smoothly to the saddle, and his hands reined the horse around. He said, "Goodbye," and lifted the horse out of the yard at a canter. In respect, Stratemeier touched his own hatbrim to the horseman loping away down the river,

then turned wearily and went into the tack shed. He stood
by the door, watching McClintock's tiny shape receding. He
put his glance on the sky, and a part of him wished to clean
from his mind the disorder past. But his mind was held by
the losses of his life, not its triumphs, and he could only see
his experience as a history of ghostly half-regret and
emptiness. Weariness thrust down against his strong back.
He lay on the dusty cot and closed his eyes.

Sometime in the course of the afternoon he found himself
sitting bolt upright, trying to identify the sound that had
disturbed him. His eyes traveled to the doorway. Within
the door, sharply silhouetted, Kathy rose on the step and
stood with a hand poised against the jamb. "It's done?"

"Will got his chance," he said. "He didn't want it that
way."

"And now—you'll move on?"

"I guess not," he said. "I guess not."

"Eric." Her hand dropped to her side; she advanced and
stood rooted in the center of the floor, her shoulder very
square, her expression very level. "Don't blame yourself for
what you had to do—or what happened twenty years ago."

His glance held hers. Nothing seemed certain, except
perhaps the fidelity in her wordless offer. She glided to the
cot and lowered herself, looking down into his face. Her
lids dropped, and he could not see what was in her eyes; he
watched her gravely, brought his hand up, and touched the
point of her chin. Presently, she touched his shoulders. Her
fingers laced together at the back of his neck, and when her
eyes lifted, there was in their depths a world beyond any
other world his own power might bring him. The pressure
of her hands grew; she came forward to him. He felt a
question lying naked in her thoughts. His eyes touched the
bleak ceiling, and when he spoke, his voice was quite low:
"I don't know."

ABOUT THE AUTHOR

Born in 1939, BRIAN GARFIELD began writing short stories at age twelve and wrote his first published novel when he was 18 (*Range Justice*, 1960). Having grown up on Southwestern ranches, he turned his literary talents to the American West and immediately established a reputation as one of the finest Western novelists of his generation.

He found time to graduate from the University of Arizona (B.A., 1959) and complete his graduate studies (M.A., 1963), to teach, to tour with a professional jazz band, and to serve in the U.S. Army and Army Reserve (1957–65). Since 1963 he has been a fulltime writer of novels, short stories, and screenplays.

Garfield has produced nearly seventy books of fiction and nonfiction, including *Death Wish*, *Hopscotch* (winner of the Edgar Award and basis for the popular film), *The Paladin*, *Wild Times* (Nominated for the American Book Award and filmed as a TV miniseries), *The Thousand-Mile War*, *Western Films*, *Kolchak's Gold*, *Relentless*, and *Tripwire*. As president of his own film company, Garfield has overseen production of two of his own properties. He is also the only person ever to have served as president of both the Mystery Writers of America and the Western Writers of America.

In short, this prolific author is very difficult to typecast. Always writing, Garfield is a frequent traveler, college lecturer, and guest on radio and television interview shows. With over 17 million copies of his books sold worldwide (in eighteen languages), Brian Garfield is currently at work on a major historical novel. He and his wife Bina live in Southern California.

Roe Richmond is one of that rare breed of Western writers whose novels continue to be read by generation after generation. In the tradition of Luke Short and Ernest Haycox, he is a storyteller of power and passion who brings back to life the authentic Old West.

Roe Richmond has these great westerns to offer you:

Elmore Leonard "should be a household name."
—*The Philadelphia Inquirer*

His characters become etched in your mind, his dialogue snaps off the page, and his keen understanding of the violent tensions between people who live on the edge will rivet you to your chair. Bantam offers you these exciting titles:

And if Western adventure is what you're after, Bantam has these tales of the frontier to offer from ELMER KELTON, one of the great Western storytellers with a special talent for capturing the fiercely independent spirit of the West:

Short Story Collections from
LOUIS L'AMOUR

"Bantam Books is the only publisher authorized to issue my short stories in book form."

—*Louis L'Amour.*